Maria Reinecke- **Living In Between**

Bibliografische Information der Deutschen Nationalbibliothek
Die Deutsche Nationalbibliothek verzeichnet diese Publikation in der Deutschen Nationalbibliografie; detaillierte bibliografische Daten sind im Internet über http//www.d-nb.de abrufbar.

ISBN: 978-3-941524-22-4
ISBN: 978-3-941524-24-8 (eBook)

1. Edition English
PalmArtPress, 2013

German Edition:
Leben in den Zwischenräumen
PalmArtPress, 2013
ISBN 978-3-941524-21-7
ISBN: 978-3-941524-23-1 (eBook)
Editor: Catharine J. Nicely
Cover Photo: Bernd Reinecke (Market Square in Pollensa, Mallorca)
Translation: Mollie Hosmer-Dillard
Printed in Germany

Pfalzburgerstr. 69, 10719 Berlin
www.palmartpress.com

Maria Reinecke

Living In Between

Translated from the German
by Mollie Hosmer-Dillard

PalmArtPress
Berlin

Prologue

Where is the beginning? Where I begin. It has always begun before me: regardless of where I begin. Putting splinters together, shreds of life, of what has been lived, trusting in pent-up pictures, thoughts, memories. How to arrange it all, follow the thread, weave a story? There is no seam for this thread. Everything is like this, and at the same time has always been completely different.

Angles of truth.

Angles of lies.

To reach the angle of eternity.

Once upon a time, there was a man who had seven sons, and the seven sons said, Father, tell us a story. So the father began, once upon a time there was a man who had seven sons, and the seven sons said, Father, tell us a story. So the father began, once upon a time there was a man...

The grown-ups are laughing; the child does not understand, he is laughing along but he sounds unsure of himself, almost sad; he would have liked to remain in the moment when they said that someone should tell a story, any story; that had been exciting, the moment when everything suddenly seemed possible, a hole appeared in the mechanical structure of things, a gap opened for the unexpected, space for freedom, vastness, adventure, and his attention was freed for the miraculous.

Once upon a time there was a man, a woman, a child. And then? A story has to be told some time. Maybe. If it is still needed then. After all, I am of Jewish descent, so there would be the story of my mother, but I don´t feel compelled to dedicate yet another monument to that perverse time. I know my luck. The story would fall into the hands of some keen director, inspiring him to construct historically accurate scenes with abhorrent swastikas; just imagine someone happening upon those images during the evening program – if only for a few seconds – fascinated by the screaming, vacant grimaces and the immaculate cut of uniforms. No. No matter how I look at it, I have no story, don't want one.

The best thing would be simply to ponder everything

like the philosopher once did, next to the fireplace, during a frosty winter in the middle of the war.

- I assume nothing, said the wise man, slippers on his feet, sitting in the armchair.

- Do I even exist? he asked himself, while others stirred the fire for him, brought food, did the laundry, and took the garbage out. What would he have done without them, thought without them?

- I am cold! I am hungry! Therefore I am?! he may have called out eventually, desperate and a bit confused. But no, he was warm and cozy, so he could think and think incessantly, until he thought so much that he thought he might just well exist.

I don't even want to think right now, can't think right now. I sit and look. At nothing in particular. At what is there. It's good that there are things to meet one's gaze, to be thought about! I look out through the high rectangle of the window. The darkness of the roofs sits on illuminated walls across from me. It advances toward me. Sensing the darkness calms me. I perceive the darkness and feel calm. Time stands still. Let it be. Sit. Look. Penetrate the moment. Be like that house over there, like that tree. No shame, no shyness, no guilt. Be, just be; without any doubt, without any sense of trepidation. My consciousness sinks, melts into my body, stretches out through my skin into the room.

Shreds of clouds, illuminated by the city, are flying along under the black sky. It's no use. Time falls upon me again. The sense of trepidation will not cease as long as I am breathing. Me. Always me. To listen within will not do, there is nobody there. To return to yourself. As if there were someone waiting who you could meet. Me, my mood unfathomable, perceptions wound into a ball, more or less chaotic.

Marie I

1. *Marie Sitting in the Kitchen*

I´m sitting in the dark kitchen on the wicker couch. The little one is sleeping. Called in sick for another week. Borrowed time. It takes time for the blood vessels to rebuild. They did both legs, taking out the brittle veins, thirty-four incisions. There were complications. The left leg was bound too tightly after the operation, the tip of the foot had already swollen up and was beginning to turn a bluish red; the professor said it was a mess, he personally was the one who freed me from the bandage and left instructions for me to be bandaged up again. Several new blue spots are starting to appear on the left foot.

"Your tissue is very thin, there´s nothing we can do about it," explained the doctor who treated me afterwards. "Just keep on wearing the compression stockings, drink lots of water and prop up your legs!"

I am propping up my legs, especially the left one, and am moving my toes in little circles. I turn on the light, pour myself a glass of water. From behind the bottle, a receipt appears, dated February 14, full of scribbles:

- *The unspeakable has to be thought, thoughts create reality; this reality gives strength*…I don´t remember what I did that day, but I have to write things down, otherwise they´ll disappear.

Everything is within my reach, telephone, notebook, coffee, books, behind the cup my notes on Whitehead.

- Who is Whitehead? someone asks me.

- A philosopher.

- When was he alive?

- 1861 to 1947.

- Ah, yes.

- Whitehead wrote the *Principia mathematica* with Russell, I add quietly.

- Oh, Bertrand Russell! Interesting, he could go on and on about anything, was very amusing at times!

It's moments like those that emptiness breaks open inside of me, filled with sadness, like a woolen blanket that suffocates everything. Tightness in my lower body makes its way up to my stomach. That has nothing to do with Whitehead of course, nor the innocent inquirer. I do not feel well generally, a little bit like being in an open field when it's hailing. It isn't just my legs. Everything's always getting stuck.

Johannes's sixth birthday is coming up, he wants to invite the whole kindergarten, difficult in the small apartment, but it will be so crowded that he'll believe they all came. No word from Christian yesterday either. I'm tired, will try to sleep.

I can't sleep, go to the nursery, sit down on Johannes's bed. He's lying on his back, arms angled up slightly. He rolls onto his side, plunging his round cheeks back into the soft pillows, licks his lips, breathes calmly and steadily. Love flows through my body. To sit here forever. I am cold. I lie down again, close my eyes, images emerge…

> … They are coming out of church, walking across the cemetery. Christian stops, leans against a bench, takes pictures with the Rollei. Johannes is still very small, he runs along the paths between the graves. His light-blue cape flashes among the crosses. Crosses everywhere, the crucified Lord.
>
> … *I'm thirsty. There was a vessel full of vinegar. They filled a sponge with vinegar, put it on a hyssop branch, and held it to his mouth. When Jesus had received the vinegar, he said: "It is finished!" He bowed his head, and relinquished his spirit…*
>
> The little rascal comes running, stops in front of them.

"Ouch, Mama, Jesus has a big ouch."

"Yes, Jesus suffers because he loves people," Marie says.

"Does he love everyone, Mama, even the bad people?" His face is pale.

"Yes, he loves everyone, even people we don't like very much."

Johannes disappears again between the graves.

Christian puts away his camera, sits down on the bench, lights a cigarette. Marie sits down next to him.

"He needs you, Christian. Every night he asks, 'Where is Papa now? Doesn't Papa love you anymore, Mama? But he still loves me, right Mama?' And he squeezes his teddy bear, tossing and turning in bed and crying, 'I want my Kistian-papa back!'"

"He'll understand someday," Christian says.

"Johannes needs you now."

"I just can't deal with this right now." Christian stares straight ahead. "I feel like I've been hauling sand from one end of the desert to the other for years…" he continues, resting his arms on his knees, ash falling on his trousers. "Sometimes I just lie there and think, there's no point anymore: Whether I get up now or not, the world will keep running alright without me."

"It could very well be that it would run more smoothly with your help! It would at least be worth a try!" Marie says, turning away.

"Oh, you have no idea! You just don't know what it's like to live with this fear, to feel so dirty and guilty. Don't you know I love Johannes, too?" Christian's voice is trembling. Marie turns back to him.

"You have to want to get over your misery, not nurse it…" she says.

"You're always telling me the same things, always the same things. I *am* trying, but then I have these hazy dreams at night…I hate him!" Christian throws the cigarette to the ground, grinds it with his heel.

"You have to forgive your father, Christian."

"Forgive, forgive, how can I ever forgive that bastard? He destroyed my life, he destroyed our life, he destroyed everything! Forgive? No way. I don't have to do anything!"

"Your hatred is destroying you, you have to…"

Christian jumps up and shouts:

“Good, I forgive him, I forgive him, happy now?”

It’s very quiet all of a sudden. Johannes! They look around. The little light-blue figure is lying behind them on the ground, between the plots.

“Johannes! Little man!”

They rush over to him. The child’s eyes are closed, his thick, fair hair framing his white face.

“Johannes!”

He opens his eyes, the blood surging back into the skin. He doesn’t know what happened, no, he didn’t fall. Christian carries him to the car. When they arrive at the hotel, Johannes is already playing with his Lego bus again.

“It’s probably this Good Friday mood in the air today…” Christian says to himself.

At some point I fall asleep.

2. *A Postcard From Afar*

Johannes is in kindergarten. They've been hammering, drilling for days in the apartment above me. You can feel the noise. Nobody minds. Most of them are out of the house during the day, and Mrs. Breyer downstairs across from me is hard of hearing anyway.

The phone rings.

"Aunt Elsa! Good Morning! Yes, Johannes is already gone."

"How are your legs?" asks the kind woman.

"I'm doing all right."

"Erich wants to know when Johannes is going to come by again to liven the place up. I could come and pick him up today."

"Thank you, Auntie, he'll be so happy!"

"Say, what's my dear sister-in-law up to, anyway? I haven't heard from her since her birthday."

"Oh, Mother's upset because you just wrote a card

and didn't call."

"Well, listen! I always end up distracting her from watching television, so I don't call anymore, really…"

"Give my love to Erich, thanks, Aunt Elsa!"

"Yes, darling, see you tonight!"

The February-March sun drifts timidly through the milky grey windowpane, blue bits of the sky can be seen between white clouds, spring is on its way, I will clean windows, at least the one in the kitchen, and plant yellow primroses, Johannes likes those. I go to bring the mail up. The heating bill from the year before last, they want another 186.17 DM; how did they come up with that amount? I´m invited to review the documents at any point after consultation with the property management, that's all I need. Amidst junk mail, a postcard:

"Dear Marie, stuck between Australia and the Antarctic, Greetings from afar! R."

Rudolf! Flakes of memories drift through my stomach, a queasy sadness, Rudolf: son of a watchmaker, never wore a watch, Rudolf Kempf, professor of mathematics, regularly confused by his dreams in the night; always looking for pure adventure on his vacations, traveling through South America and East Asia or camping in Africa, with the secret hope that something might happen to him; now he was at the ends of the earth. Stupid card, white steamboat in the blue sea, masses of ice behind it. I don't feel like thinking about Rudolf, am happy that I can listen to Santana again without crying. But it had been short and sweet.

3. *The Mathematician*

It was a Wednesday. They met in the university cafeteria. He sits down at her table; they smile at each other, directness, yes, rare in these latitudes… Spain! Things are totally different there. His eyes lock with hers; he speaks Spanish quite well, is in Madrid regularly, Seville, Saragossa, for conferences, research…

"You're a mathematician?"

"Yes, can you tell?" He laughs. "My name's Rudolf, Rudolf Kempf, I'm on the 6th floor. Do you work here too?"

"Over there, in the philosophy department…"

"Oh, a philosopher!" His eyes flash with amusement. "I have to pass on that, unfortunately. I prefer to keep to safer terrain; philosophy is too difficult for me, especially since, it unfortunately doesn't achieve anything." He grins and shoves a sizable piece of pork cutlet into his mouth. Marie´s pulse is strong.

"It's certainly true that two sheep plus two sheep equals four sheep, but this kind of truth just isn't enough," she says and is annoyed with herself at the same time. Silly enough to want to have a conversation with a mathematician about mathematics as a non-mathematician. The thing about the sheep was obviously completely off the mark. Mathematics works because of absolute abstraction, it formulates truths in which sheep and goats play no role at all. Her head is spinning, she pours herself some water.

He smirks:

"With or without sheep, mathematics is generally quite a reasonable, respectable subject with which you can't do too much damage, don't you think?"

Of course she agrees, but that isn't what this is about. The lanky elegance of his posture, his vaguely Indian profile, the soft glow from his dark brown eyes, his resonant, almost husky voice that trails upwards after every sentence as if it were constantly posing questions, the deep wrinkles in his cheeks: She likes the whole man, and it's building like a storm inside her.

"The certainty and accuracy of mathematics, the whole scientific meticulousness applies to realms that are unfortunately not existentially relevant to humanity," Marie says finally.

- Why can't I just enjoy the situation, bathe in the

gaze of this unusual man and be quiet? she thinks and takes a sip of water.

It's noisy, the rattling of silverware, glasses and dishes, unrecognizable smells all around her, people all over looking for places to sit, holding trays full of all kinds of neatly arranged food.

"Ah well, man is and remains an equation with too many unknowns!" Rudolf says with an indifferent smile, mashing a potato.

Blood rushes to her brain, she hates aphorisms.

"Even after the scientists have measured, analyzed, classified everything, there's still a lot left over… Subjectivity has to be included in the discussion, otherwise it will be lost…reason takes everything seriously: *The fairies dance and Christ is being crucified…"* Marie hears herself say, strangely incoherently, her heart pounding in her chest.

Rudolf looks up, surprised.

"Yes, that's how Whitehead expresses it at one point," she adds. She is blushing.

"The mathematician and scientist Alfred North Whitehead? I think he lost his son, maybe that's where his strange cosmology comes from, but, like I said, I'm not a philosopher."

Rudolf's voice has lost its conversational tone. Marie spoons her potato soup, filled with lots of sausage slices, sets the spoon down, tries to catch her breath:

"Maybe one should a consider the possibility that someone who is deeply involved with absolute abstraction might one day start to tune into new and surprising ways of thinking, experiencing a dimension of reality that he had never noticed before, had not been open to, or simply had not thought possible. His new way of looking at things doesn't come from any lack or want but rather from an abundance of awareness." Her voice sounds relaxed now, the sentences flow of their own volition.

Rudolf stops chewing.

"Philosophy just can't make any rationally justifiable statements about the world," he counters promptly.

"Oh, a little philosopher after all!" she says, smiling triumphantly, enjoying his presence now.

They continue to eat in silence. Suddenly he leans towards her, touches her arm, comes very close, his face is serious.

"There is no answer for man, and definitely no salvation," he says quietly.

Such incredible nearness. Marie's heart is pounding, her breath is caught in her chest, impulses from within are emanating charged density, something is encircling both of them, time coagulates.

"Is this seat taken?" A young man sets his full tray onto the table, sits down.

"I have to go," Marie says and gives Rudolf her address.

"I'll call you! I live in Spandau. Adios!" he calls after her.

When Marie sits down in the car she is weak in the knees; she surrenders herself to the flow of traffic as if in a trance, runs up to the kindergarten; Günther is sitting on the terrace with the last three children; the teacher with grey curls is slicing apples, arranging them in a circle on a plate, the children are taking them.

"We're going to eat them all up!" Alex beams, his cheeks are full, he points to the big bowl of apples behind him.

"I have a little sister! I've got a little sister!" Nadja announces excitedly.

"That's great!" Marie gives the girl a hug. She is out of breath and apologizes for being late.

"Why on earth do the mothers always come running up feeling guilty? The children are having a good time here!" Günther, who insists on being called by his first name, sounds almost offended. As if the children couldn't possibly be missing out on anything with him!

Johannes has already put on his backpack and is saying goodbye to everyone and falling into Marie's arms.

"Goodbye, Günther, and thanks for everything!" Marie waves at the friendly man, says goodbye to the children and walks hand in hand with Johannes back through the park to the street.

"Mama, are we still going to visit Aunt Elsa?" the boy asks.

"No, Aunt Elsa is at the hospital today with Uncle Erich."

"Hopefully he has good doctors there, Mama."

"Do you know what? We'll wash the car!" Marie says.

"Oh no! Well, ok, but I get to hold the hose! Mama, Alex says that our car isn't a real car."

"That's right, our car is a Beetle!"

"No, Mama, don´t joke around! Alex's father has a big Jeep; he can drive around the whole world with it! I want to have a Jeep, too, when I grow up."

They get into the car and drive away.

4. *Finest Threads*

The next morning, a letter "For Marie Michaelsen" in the mailbox. Marie skims through the lines, half sentences written in flowing ink:

"...Comunicación incompleta...

As far as the stars and yet quite near.

Moments of enchantment...

I could barely endure...

My senses filled with sounds...

Inversion, I am looking inward...

Corazón tranquílo! R. K."

She takes Johannes to kindergarten, sits in a café at the Steubenplatz, grasping the letter firmly in her hand.

"A cup of coffee and a yoghurt, please." The coffee spills as she's stirring; her tears as she's reading. The finest threads have just been spun, the fear of ripping them.

A young couple sits in front of her. The man orders two big breakfasts and a heap of croissants to go with it. Neither says a word, are looking and chewing away from each other.

-Rudolf Kempf!

Marie whispers the name to herself like a magic spell. Desire, agitation, overexcitement run rampant inside her. Take your time, be close to yourself, be close to the other, to want to lose yourself, to not be allowed to lose yourself, fear of too much, fear of too little. The handkerchief wet. Corazón tranquílo!

-Rudolf! Is he the one? Is he finally the one?

The young woman in front of her stands up, goes to the bathroom. She looks pretty with her ponytail and tight T-shirt that accentuates her ample bosom. The man continues to read the paper spread out before him. Did they quarrel? But why?

-Rudolf! He's probably sailing, playing tennis or hiking up glaciers; his skin seems permanently tanned. She herself doesn't care for sports. Only likes to ride her bicycle.

- Rudolf! Who is he really? Be quiet, heart!

Snatches of piano music from the speaker above her accompany the silent sequence of events outside: a young woman maneuvers a stroller across the street – the wind blows up her wide, beige coat, she will surely lift up off the ground at any moment now – then backwards up the steps to the gift shop, the door of the shop opens, someone is helping from inside.

9.30 a.m. Marie has to leave. Matthias is giving a presentation about Leibniz's monads today, we'll see. Marie's eyes feel swollen, it doesn't matter, she has a cold after all. She pays. And runs. No time. Never really any time…

Socrates would stand in the marketplace all day and let the truth be borne slowly into every single one; step by step…

She hurries to the car, starts it, drives up Reichsstraße.

-…Truth is set into reality and therefore has to be possible; truth prohibits the impossible; because what is real is happening, after all, and what is happening is not impossible, her thoughts make the usual rounds as she drives around Theodor-Heuss-Platz… - Everything happens in every moment, nothing happens in isolation; the slightest breath has an effect on the inexhaustible process of the universe… She is smiling to herself… Me, too; which at the very least gives me a certain importance, she thinks lightheartedly and turns into Kaiserdamm.

In the afternoon Johannes brings home his friends, Max and Andreas, spoiled twins from the neighborhood. They eat fresh slices of cucumber at Marie's and even stay the night, despite the fact that they never touch any greens at home and almost never spend the night anywhere else.

Marie sits at the round table in the kitchen with the children, the wooden crucifix in the middle, a souvenir from Anne from Spain. Both are staring steadfastly at the cross.

"Who's that?" Max asks.

"Jesus Christ," Marie says.

"But that hurts!" the brother butts in.

"Yes, it hurts a lot."

"Jesus is the son of God," Johannes explains.

The boys stop eating.

"Jesus doesn't hit anyone, he is really good and likes everyone, even the bad people," Johannes adds.

The twins continue to eat in silence. They seem to accept the matter for now. Then the three of them go off to play.

5. *Nicolai's Church*

Saturday. Marie wakes up early, the first birds are chirping, spring is here. Rudolf! Everything is so fresh, so new! Overflowing! Life! It's about time! He still hasn't called.

In the morning she takes Johannes on a trip to the old town of Spandau. They race each other in the market place. Bells are ringing. A crowd of people in front of Nicolai's Church. A wedding carriage pulls up, the bride smiles expertly, the groom has lost all facial expression because of the excitement; it's chilly, they're riding with the top open, wearing almost nothing, they'll catch their deaths of cold!

Back home, Marie is preparing the food, sweeping the balcony, filling the flower boxes with new soil, the sun is breaking through. Johannes brings his Legos outside. Rudolf! When will he get in touch with her? Corazón tranquílo!

The phone is ringing! Marie runs over, picks up the

receiver breathlessly.

"This is Kempf, Rudolf Kempf! I just wanted to find out whether you really exist! "

"Yes, alive and kicking!" Suns exploding in her body.

He managed to get two tickets for the St. Matthew Passion at Nicolai's Church, left aisle, tomorrow, Sunday, 6 p.m.! Would she like to go with him? Of course she would.

"I'll cry," she whispers.

"I imagine it will be contagious," he whispers back.

Marie is breathing shallowly, listening intently as he stumbles from one sentence to the next:

"I've been thinking about you the whole time. I felt very close to myself in your presence, I haven't felt that way for such a long time…"

She feels that gravity has been suspended.

"I'm looking forward to it so much!"

"Me, too! Adios!"

6. *St. Matthew Passion and Fado*

Sunday. Johannes is at Christian's. Marie's hair, face, body are joining together to a beautiful unity, black skirt, tapered suit jacket, pumps, slender legs between them. She parks the car on Moritzstraße.

There he is! Tall, almost thin, bent slightly forward, hands in his pockets, his eyes clinging to the shop window. Hasn't he seen her? Why isn't he coming towards her? Something dampens her joy, cotton in her stomach, she rushes towards him, he slowly turns to her. His voice comes from far away.

"...I wasn't expecting this. How beautiful you are, all in black, see, it comes naturally to you. I'm wearing brown trousers and a red scarf, they don't go together at all, I just didn't think about it..."

"But aren't you still looking forward to it?"

"Yes, I am. But after our phone call yesterday, all of a sudden this pain shot through my back, the doctor says lumbago, I've never had it before, I could hardly move, but absolutely did not want to cancel…I let them give me an injection…Yes, you really got under my skin."

His laughter sounds forced.

"I'm in quite a bit of pain, you have to believe me."

Finally he takes her arm.

"The Passion is almost three hours long, you can't sit for that long, especially in this cold," Marie says.

Rudolf insists on staying; he doesn't know the St. Matthew Passion, simply hasn't been interested in it before and wanted to make up for it today. They start in the direction of the church. He walks like a wooden board. When he reaches his seat, he kneels down with his torso stiff, manages the final distance contorted with pain, collapsing into his seat.

Choir and orchestra fill the sanctuary. The instruments are being tuned. Expectant suspense in the high chamber. Marie is looking forward to the opening chorus. Unfortunately the conductor, with all his strained eagerness, is lacking one thing: agility. So choir and orchestra drag, plodding along like mush. But Bach's brilliance shines through despite all this. *…Oh innocent Lamb of God, slaughtered upon the cross…* Her thoughts and emotions oscillate between the Passion and the man next to her. Unfortunately it's completely inappropriate to take his hand or put her head on his shoulder, so she only secretly glances at his smart profile next to her from time to time, admiring the tender ears and the full lips. His eyes slide over to her though his head doesn't move, a hint of a smile, also not appropriate in the middle of the black and white clad, motionless Spandau audience.

...Truly I say to you, one of you shall betray me... Is it I? Is it I, Lord, is it I? Then all the disciples abandoned him and fled...Oh mortal, bewail your great sin...

Intermission.

He wants to walk a little, struggles to his feet. They fight their way through the crowded aisles, escape outside where they meet an unpleasant wind.

"Judas is actually a poor sod," Rudolf says. "I don't really know anything about it, of course. This Jesus does say that everything is destined to happen this way, but woe to the person who actually really betrays him in the end. So Judas is damned from the outset, if you want to stick with the terminology, he doesn't have any chance at all."

They stop in an alcove. Marie is silent.

"Over the last few years, I've used a lot of people as they came into my life; I've often felt like a traitor," Rudolf says and puts his hand on her shoulder. She feels chilly and dizzy: her stomach empty, a cold coming on, this man next to her and the moving story of the man from Nazareth.

They walk back toward the church.

"I've heard the St. Matthew Passion many times, and now you have an impression. We should go, it's cold…" Marie says.

He wants to stay until the end.

When they emerge from the church, Spandau is deserted. Finally they find an Italian place. Fried peppers, zucchini, eggplants, pane, Chianti, si. *Ma-ma-ma-Mama-Mari-i-a-a-Ma-ma-ma...*music playing behind them, with the cozy room temperature even the warbling chorus is somewhat comforting.

Rudolf perches strained on the cushioned bench opposite her, he can't stop looking at her.

"Cheers. To us, Marie!" His voice sounds husky, he touches her wrist. The wine tastes good. "When Saint Peter weeps bitterly and the rooster crows…I cried, too, at that part," he says softly.

The St. Matthew Passion is ultimately an expression of profound religious faith, Marie was wondering the whole time how he would deal with this; she starts in on a long-winded explanation:

"Yes, even the evangelist shows emotion at that point, his usually rather distanced account of the events in secco recitatives…"

"I've told a lot of lies in my life. You just don't understand that at all, do you, Marie? Have you ever told a lie?" he interrupts her.

"What gives you the impression I haven't? I've told lies, too…" Why is he pushing her away? Why is he creating distance when they were trying to find intimacy? The finest threads…

"Marie, how have you managed to keep so much light inside you? Most things undermine the power of light… Oases want to be well protected, the drought is merciless once it starts…" He sounds strangely solemn.

"Doesn't everybody carry their oases and deserts inside them?" she says, just to say something.

For a while they carry on eating without a speaking a word.

"I have a whole wall full of records, popular music, a lot from South America", he suddenly continues in a cheerful tone. "And fado. The first time I heard fado, in Portugal, it almost tore me apart. Do you know fado?"

"No."

"Hits from the 50s and 60s, too, ridiculous, right? *Hot sand and a lost land…*" he signs shyly and takes her hand.

"What do you expect from a mathematician, Marie, what do you think I can be for you?"

She looks at him, astonished.

"Yes, I'm somewhat uncertain," he says in a low voice, his gaze drifting past her.

-Why is this man talking such nonsense? Marie thinks while the all-too-well-known feelings of disappointment creep up her throat.

He takes her hand:

"Oh, it doesn't have to mean what it might normally mean," he says smilingly and kisses her fingertips. "Damn it, I can't just sit here!" he blurts out.

They laugh. It's all very simple. They both just need time. Tranquil heart.

7. *Time Happens*

The doorbell rings. My leg has fallen asleep, I hobble to the door: Mrs. Breyer in a light grey ladies' suit and wide-brimmed hat that covers half her face, matching shoes and handbag.

"Mrs. Michaelsen, good, you're home. I have to go see the doctor now. My son's coming over later. Did you get a bill as well? I'm supposed to pay another hundred DM! Well, my son can check on that later. Tomorrow they're going to turn off the water for the whole day, all day without water! So who are these people that are moving in upstairs?"

I don't know but can reassure her that only the hot water will be turned off, only between 11 a.m. and 1 p.m. A car honks.

"Someone's honking! See, I do hear well! My son always says that I'm hard of hearing. I heard that honking very clearly. That's my taxi, goodbye!" Mrs. Breyer jumps into the elevator.

I return to sit in the kitchen, from my seat I can see Mrs. Breyer climbing into the car. She can't close the door. The driver gets out, walks around the car, closes the door, drives off. During this time the traffic has backed up on the one-way street.

I'm sucking on a piece of toast, perusing last year's calendar, the page for January has been torn out:

February 10: Unrest, weakness. Next semester Spinoza: amor dei intellectualis. March 3: Johannes's birthday! Pick up cake, blow up balloons. March 12: Met Rudolf Kempf, mathematician, in the cafeteria...

- Another year has passed, always this unrest, time is flying, carrying me off somewhere I don't want to go. I have to brace myself against this tyranny, expose it as nothingness, this bloated triumvirate of time: The future that doesn't exist but surrenders to the blind plummeting of the hazily defined present, falling and falling, brushing the imaginary point of the present and inevitably emptying into a past that doesn't exist either, where it disappears once and for all. What is time without me, actually? I help it exist, I give it permanence in the here and now, it has to go through me; I give its indifferent, anonymous vastness order, structure, meaning. Destroy the undefined future in every moment, transform it into reality. I, too, take mercy on the past by remembering things after they've happened; only in me does the past continue to have an effect, it exists through me. It is not time that can harm me: No, it is rather events that besiege me from all sides, allow me no rest, there's always something happening…

I don't feel well, close my eyes, lean back, everything is spinning behind my closed eyelids.

- ...At some point, an immense process began or was begun, what do I know. In any case, as an inexorable fact of the universe it has begun, and I, bound to a world that is happening at the same time, am involved in it, myself a kind of event amidst events, a center that the world is clinging to, that the world has to pass through. In every moment something is put into effect inside me, on me, around me, my being is the life of billions of cells inside me that continuously cease to be and come into being, millions of life centers keep my organism running, something continues to happen relentlessly: I am, I become, I am, I become, am, become, am, become, until at some point the becoming has been fulfilled and the being has caught up with me, death: being and decaying in the same moment…

The phone is ringing. I open my eyes, sit up:

"Grüß dich!" Christian's familiar franconian

salutation. “Couldn’t call, felt rotten. It’s better today. Uschi’s helping me a lot at the moment. “

“Uschi?”

“Yes, she’s new to the group. Incest victim, too. Really bad, well, I don’t want to burden you with this…” he mumbles.

“Go on.” I’m glad to hear from him.

“Well, it’s just unimaginable: The father screws her for years until at eighteen she finally moves out, then he goes for the little sister, she finally reports him, the guy’s taken into custody. During the trial the mother tries to cover up for the brute and says her daughter is lying, so the sister kills herself. Uschi is totally devastated, of course she feels she’s to blame for her sister’s death because she left her alone in that mess; she knew what her sister was going through at home; and then her own story. I’m trying to help her, to show her that I understand…”

“It’s Johannes’s birthday next week! The children will be here at 3:30,” I interrupt him.

“Oh yeah, yeah, what day is today?” Christian sounds very nervous.

“Thursday.”

“I mean, what date?”

“The 26th.”

“Good, there’s still some time! I’ll come by on

Monday to drop everything off. Our self-help group is having a big carnival party on Tuesday …"

"They're having a carnival party in Johannes's kindergarten on Tuesday, too. The parents have been invited as well. It's a shame that you won't be able make it again this year."

"I was there last year," Christian raises his voice.

"Don't forget, February only has 28 days."

"Yeah, yeah. How are your legs, by the way? I could stop by for a bit later on."

"Okay, see you then!" I hang up, am feeling better, will wash my hair.

I washed my hair. The window can wait, I am sitting comfortably right now, a bottle of water in front of me; I should drink more; would love to go have a nice breakfast with Irene again, like we did last year…

8. *Café Hardenberg*

Marie and Irene sit in the Café Hardenberg. Irene loves the place, enjoys the smoky, student noblesse with the sofas and their worn fabric and leather, the creaky parquet floors, the yellowed posters, not to mention the plentiful breakfast on huge plates, and Beethoven, Mahler, Tchaikovsky playing in the background dramatically. Irene herself never really had an education, she ran away from home when she was very young, she never felt like going back to school to get her high school diploma, she became a nurse, married a doctoral student, supported him through his dissertation, had high hopes for her son who, from the look of things, wasn't going to get his high school diploma either.

A big breakfast for two is served, a veritable feast with orange juice and sparkling wine.

"Incredible!" Irene's voice rings out through the room. Grins from the table next to us.

“So, what’s your Klaus doing in the States?” Marie asks.

“He’s been calling regularly, calls are dirt-cheap over there, you know, he hasn’t seen much of Washington yet, sits at the university all day, or so he says. He’s also already bought a car, we absolutely have to go and visit him in the summer, Jan doesn’t want to, you know, those two don’t really like each other. Well, a few weeks alone wouldn’t hurt Klaus and me either!”

This woman’s face is gaunt, aged much too quickly, but now it is glowing, she is proud of her intelligent husband who works his way from research contract to research contract in hopes of some day being offered a professorship somewhere. But who would possibly want to hire an education academic whose specialty is the democratization of school systems in postwar Berlin? So she continues to work as a receptionist at the urologist.

“And how are things with you?” Irene asks while chewing.

“Same as usual. Christian’s therapy doesn’t seem to be working.”

“You know what I don’t get?” Irene leans back. “How someone can suddenly have memories about something that he didn’t have an inkling about before!” she says and crosses one leg over the other.

"Didn't Christian always use to talk about his sheltered childhood? And then, suddenly, his father is supposed to be this beast!"

Marie is taking a bite from a crunchy baguette with ham hanging over both sides, a piece of meat gets caught in her throat. Irene won't let go:

"First his mother dies, then his photo exhibition falls through. It's normal for someone to be down under those circumstances! But then, as soon as he goes into therapy he remembers a thing like that!"

Marie is silent. Irene takes a slurp of her sparkling wine, will stop at nothing:

"Maybe his memories are just fantasies or flights of imagination, what do we know about what the therapists suggest? I've heard the craziest things. They can awaken all sorts of stuff in you through hypnosis. They only stop once you admit to being the leader of a satanic cult or something…" Irene takes a cigarette, starts smoking. Marie feels slightly queasy…

….Christian comes from the child's room looking pale, lights a cigarette, his hands are trembling.

"What's wrong?" Marie asks, alarmed.

"I said good night to Johannes, we put his bear to sleep. I'm scared." Christian sits down on the sofa.

"My father often used to tuck me in at night. I used to have a little bear, too, back then, he only had one ear, my father used to treat it like a real animal. He'd read stories to us and then lie next to me and wait until I was asleep." Christian gets up, walks to the window slowly, stands there like column, staring fixedly at the February night, his voice strange all of a sudden:

"Then, one night, everything was different. I felt something hard in my back, my father was breathing strangely, his hand was grabbing me, it was horrible, I didn't understand what my father… I only knew that it wasn't right, I was ashamed and afraid, every night…"

"Just imagine if his father is innocent!" Irene continues, nibbling on the Esrom cheese.

Marie needs to cough, a crumb is stuck in her windpipe, she turns red, drinks some orange juice. Irene pats her back.

"Say something!"

"No, Christian's never talked about hypnosis, it's not that. I don't know. Let's talk about something else!"

"True, no man is worth worrying about. You should

be glad you're not married!" Irene says, blowing blue smoke from her nose and mouth and stubbing out the cigarette with a pointed index finger.

The two women now devote themselves entirely to the sumptuous plates with decadent fruit arrangements, the fabulous baguettes, and the whole wheat rolls sitting behind them to top it all off.

A good-looking man in his forties with shining, silver hair enters the room, The New York Times under his arm. A table in the left corner is being cleared, perfect, he sits down. What was moments ago merely an angle in the room is now a glorified vanishing point where all eyes converge. His way of sitting is skillfully sexy, he doesn't look up, assumes a natural posture and starts reading, the transition is maybe a little too quick. The waitress rushes over, his lips form a brief order, she whizzes away, once more he becomes engrossed in the front page, completely content all by himself, a monad in the room, in the universe.

"He looks great!" Irene says with a rapt look in her eyes. "Artist, literary man, architect?" she whispers, thank God, quietly.

Soon, a young man with a mop of curly hair and a purple scarf appears, approaches the inapproachable one, puts down his backpack. The wonderful man looks up, rises, hugs the young one tenderly, both sit down slowly, solemnly entranced.

"It's just like I told you, all the interesting-looking men are gay! We just don't exist for them!" Irene turns back to Marie with disappointment, while Mahler's Symphony Number 1 pours through the room, Marcia Funebre, Brother John in minor.

"Something's the matter with you," Irene says after a while with expert's eye and full mouth. It's no use, Marie has to mention Rudolf, even though there's hardly anything worth mentioning.

"A mathematician! Of all the people!" Irene exclaims and swallows audibly. Smirks from the table next to them again, four young women. Then Irene takes aim discreetly but directly:

"Have you guys …"

"No, no..."

"Okay, and how old is he?" she wants to know, as if she were asking for a criminal's description.

"He's probably around 50."

"Well, then, have fun!" Irene crosses her arms across her flat chest. "I once heard that in France the Bourbaki group, or something like that, doesn't admit mathematicians over 50 years of age. Mathematicians are supposed to be intellectually sterile, but you'll keep him busy." Irene cuts away the top of her egg with a skillful whack, pauses for a moment: “Oh, it would be so nice to really fall in love again!” she sighs and puts a pristine slice of banana in her mouth.

In that moment Irene’s beauty descends upon her, lays down on her copper hair, floods her small face; the ruby glow of her earrings melts into the freckles on her delicate nose and gets caught in her orange-tinted lips.

“We haven’t been to the cinema in ages,” Marie says.

“Yes, *Out of Africa*!” Irene exclaims excitedly, and they set a date for the following week.

9. *Window Cleaning*

I am cleaning the window. The only good thing about these new buildings is that you don't need a ladder to do it. I fill a bowl with soapy water, take the rubber gloves, and start cleaning.

It's lunchtime; the pizzeria on the corner is getting crowded. In a window across the street, the curtains open slightly, a woman's naked body appears, the head half-turned away, the woman smiles into the room, flash, five times, six times, new pose at the other end of the curtain, her hair is pinned up, she tilts her head toward her left shoulder, the curtain closes again.

I lean on the table. The woman's flesh has gotten to me, lingers in my senses – warm, fragrant skin, wonderful breasts, heavy as bells. Sometimes I see myself in the mirror, perceive my body like a stranger's, overwhelmed by its nakedness, in awe of the lust that is hidden within.

I begin with the outside window. Someone knocks

on the front door. A plumber, whether we have any wet spots here...

"What?"

"We had some flooding upstairs, I just wanted to ask whether anything has come through into your bathroom."

I go look:

"No, everything's fine!"

The man is already at the elevator.

I keep working. I can only reach the corners of the window on tiptoes. Incredible strain on the fresh scars. Way too exhausting, the whole thing! Anger and frustration slosh through my stomach.

Just to have sex again, to catch a tasty young man, like last summer, in front of the department store, the black-haired troubadours from the Andes with carpets on their shoulders, a little exoticism on Wilmersdorferstraße, a little girl with braids and a red flower in her hair sitting on a green ball among them, there, the handsome one with the bunch of mussels, the right ratio of sadness in his face, woman lets a 10 DM bill fly into the box, blows kisses to the one with soft eyes, the boys always get something, even from the mothers-in-law in Neukölln, they sing so beautifully, fight for their people, they just shoot them over there. I'm taking aim at the shell rattler, he doesn't believe it, looks away, looks over again, smiles, aha, understood, go over to him, name's Marie, you, Winston, delighted about my Spanish, has been in Germany for two weeks, music on the street, to send money to his sick mother, homesickness, alone, isn't that hard, nothing comes easily in this life says the one with black-curls, melancholic tone, not bad, why not indulge a poor musician, Johannes is at Christian's tonight, let's go for dinner tonight, my treat, gracias, gaze shines wistfully, 8 p.m. at Savigny-Platz, he's hungry, doesn't care what as long as it's a lot, German restaurant, fried potatoes with a pork steak hanging over onto the table cloth, beer, eats and eats, raw onions to go with it, will definitely stink later on, finally full, in the apartment, first a shower, pitch the camp, Adonis in a bath towel, shaking all over with arousal, has been so long, it will be quick, he says, does it, but then immediately again and again, okay, the boy is happy, sleep, once more at dawn, heavens, how did he get into my bed, make coffee, subway fare, would like to see you again, no, can't do it, have husband and child, have to go to the university, *adios*, Ramikuna, probably should have taken the one with the charango after all…

Done. The sky sits in the middle of the room. Time and time again, a miracle, such a clean window. I sit down on the rattan sofa, drink water, legs up. When was the dear professor's postcard actually stamped? End of January, so he should be back in Berlin by now, could call him, even though after our last phone call it didn't seem like there was anything more to say. He'd just returned from a conference in Beijing:

"Hi, it's me! How's the flower been all this time without the mathematician?"

"Rudolf!"

"Yes, so there I was on the other side of the world again and nothing really happened. How is the philosopher?" Without waiting for an answer, he says with a sigh: "Ah, Marie, we are a real binomial."

"To the *n* power?"

"No, to the 'root of *n*'. By the way, I'm not gay; so looks like it's more a case of sexual inexperience or just no talent for eroticism, whatever, that just means eating humble pie." He was even considering marrying again; this constant loneliness was really unnerving, and he wasn't getting any younger, it would be better to be with someone.

"So is there anyone?" I ask.

"Oh, Marie, there's always someone."

Why had he called? Even in hindsight it just wasn't clear.

I try to sit comfortably, not that easy on this basketwork despite all the cushions, eat another piece of toast, dial Irene's number; her big mouth would be good for me now, let it ring for a long time, nobody home. Shame, would have liked to have told her about the clean window. Irene appreciates stuff like that. And it's her day off today, too. Anne isn't home either, in Japan for two weeks.

Aunt Elsa calls, she and Erich are going to bring Johannes over tonight, a walk would do them good before the evening program, thanks, Aunt Elsa.

10. *Water Instead of Wine*

"I fell for your bright eyes right away," Rudolf says when Marie visits him in his apartment for the first time. They sit on big leather cushions; the lights dimmed, Satie in the background, glasses and mineral water on the low table between them; exotic souvenirs hanging on the walls; in between them paintings and drawings from artists in Berlin and children's drawings by his sons. Rudolf's back is better.

"I live apart from my family," he remarks off-handedly. "At some point my wife just couldn't stand the way I smelled any longer. So I moved out. She stayed in the house with the kids. And it's okay. We get along very well, celebrate Christmas together, each with their current partners, and I'm there every Sunday, too." He goes to get a bottle of Bordeaux and black olives from the kitchen. "Wine thickens the blood, but we should have a sip now." He puts the bottle on the table. They keep drinking water.

Then he shows her around his orderly kingdom, to which the bedroom does not seem to belong: the wooden double bed stands next to the door, the room is lined with low cabinets, a piano is squeezed between bookshelves, curtains with an indeterminable pattern and creases that look shrink-wrapped barricade the window. He doesn't mind very much, it doesn't matter anyway, when you live alone, Rudolf explains and closes the door. "I'd rather you talk about yourself. I want to know everything about you." He puts his arm around her.

"Not now," Marie says. His presence so close to her arouses her.

"What did you mean the other day about the ratio that penetrates the irrational?" Rudolf asks, his voice vibrating. He holds her tightly. Marie remains silent, enjoys the touch.

"Wait," he says, goes to the record cabinet, puts on Santana's *Earth's Cry Heaven's Smile*, walks back slowly. "For you," he whispers, and they finally sink into the suede couch, the sound of the electric guitar in their stomachs, sucking on each other like two people dying of thirst. She thinks he smells good.

11. *Mother's Call*

The kitchen is just gleaming. Could actually give my mother a call, no, not now. I wonder if I was abused as a child too. I can hardly remember my childhood, let alone my father.

"You should be glad you don't have a father, it saves you a lot of trouble," my mother used to say.

Some nights I would dream that boys with bald heads and pinched mouths would try to kiss me and that I was afraid and disgusted. Then there was this story with the children's home. I call my mother after all:

"Ah, my daughter! How's my grandchild?"

"Thanks, Johannes is..."

"So, what's up?"

"I just cleaned the kitchen window..."

"You should be careful with your legs, we don't want any complications!"

I take a deep breath: "Mother, I wanted to ask you...

you told me that once when I was three years old I came home very distraught and was covering my face with my hands, what exactly had happened?"

"What do I know? That was ages ago. Why do you want to know this all of a sudden?" she asks defensively.

"The thing with Christian, could it be that I also…"

"Nonsense, your Christian, he's bonkers," she interrupts me. "You've got problems. Hagemann – such a nice person. Besides, what's the point. Children have always been abused, and who cared during the war? I saw with my own eyes how they pounced on children and women. What does it matter if a father gropes around a little?"

"Sexual abuse is a crime, the victims' suffering…"

"Suffering. What do you know about suffering! Today everybody runs to their psychiatrists and blames their own failures on their parents, give me a break! We didn't have any help back then either, we had to find out on our own how to cope with our crappy lives!"

"I'm sorry, I…"

"Yeah, let's just forget it. You had so much you wanted to get done in the last few weeks; what about your work on that…what's his name again, I just can't remember the name, White-something…?"

"Whitehead."

"Yes, yes, my god, who cares about that? Why don't you write about Kant again, at least everybody knows him. And your Christian, he should be working. Condemning his own father but taking the money, ah well, whatever! By the way, I'm going on a bus tour to Switzerland soon, I've always wanted to see Switzerland, such a nice, cultivated country, and I still have my wits about me, thank God. I have to go to the hairdresser's now, bye!" She hangs up.

12. *Stubborn Facts*

Marie and Rudolf meet at the back entrance to the Gardens of Charlottenburg Palace. Tourists don't come here. They walk in a tight embrace as if they had been born this way.

"Ah, Marie, where is fate leading us?" Rudolf wonders aloud.

"That makes it sound like we're flagellates in the currents." Marie smiles and tilts her head to look at him.

"Yes, sometimes I feel like a flagellate, happy and free." His tone is still serious.

"I don't think that you're like a flagellate, and I also don't think that a flagellate is free and happy," Marie jokingly retorts.

"Why not? Flagellates swim and swim and are probably convinced they're free, maybe they're even sort of happy, what do we know?" Now he sounds coquettish.

“The flagellate just follows the current blindly, doesn’t know anything about happiness,” Marie continues.

“But we just follow the current, too…”

“We can always choose to swim against the current, Rudolf, dear,” she interrupts with a facetious face.

“Yes, but that requires a lot of courage and strength, my dear Marie,” he says just as facetiously and hugs her tightly.

They laugh and cross the meadow. Suddenly Rudolf stops:

“What’s the story with Christian?”

“When I was pregnant, his mother died. Christian became severely depressed, went into therapy, and discovered that he had been abused by his father as a child,” Marie says quietly, looks down, noticing Rudolf’s elegant shoes… They walk on slowly.

“I thought this kind of thing only happened to girls,” he says after a brief silence.

…His shoes are made of smooth brown leather and have a sporty elegance, making it unclear where he got them. The brown-green corduroys fall loosely onto the instep, at the back casually over the flat heel. Marie looks up at him; a large-patterned plaid woolen shirt, fleecy with calm, harmonious colors peeks out from the half-opened brown leather jacket: demurely dapper, but somehow sexy…

"Do you know his father?" she hears Rudolf ask.

"Yes, former chief physician, attractive, educated, amusing, nice…" she answers mechanically…Most men she's known have only worn jeans and turtleneck jerseys…

"How are you supposed to take something like that?" Rudolf gulps. "I mean, when my sons were young I caressed them, bathed them, rubbed them with baby oil, cuddled with them, kidded around with them, and romped around. That was certainly sensual, the whole thing, my wife was much more reserved. My sons still hug me today, we're affectionate with each other, but never in my life would I have thought that something like that…" He pauses, clears his throat.

"Your sons were just lucky," Marie says as they pass His Majesty's teahouse.

"And then what happened?" Rudolf asks cautiously.

"Christian's state worsened so much that he couldn't go on working at his job as an art teacher, and at some point he moved into his studio."

Marie breaks away from his embrace, runs ahead to the bridge, stops in the middle of it, looks across the pond with the swans towards the axial fountain and onto the silhouette of the palace behind it. A murder of crows darkens the sky. Rudolf follows, his back still injured, stands behind her, wraps his arms around her. Moments of erotic enchantment. Then they take the narrow path along the edge of the pond. Three sleeping ducks pitch and toss on the water, their heads nestled deep into their feathers.

"You can't take a nap now, in the middle of the day! Look how beautiful the world is!" Marie shouts to them. But the animals don't care about her, their heads are tucked away and they drift up and down on the short waves, back and forth.

"What do you think, where should the bed go?" Rudolf says suddenly; his voice is husky. "I'm rearranging everything at my place, maybe I should buy a new bed? And the piano? That could actually go into the salon. It just has to be tuned, but it works fine."

Marie pauses, they still haven't slept together and he's already making plans for a shared bedroom.

"And what if we're not a good fit at all?" she asks, as if she were talking about two Lego blocks.

"Well, we're not all that bad," he whispers, stops, takes her head in his hands, gently runs his lips over her mouth, waits until she opens it, and for a small eternity they sink into the hot wetness of each other's mucous membranes.

A jogger wheezes past them. They continue walking.

"Stubborn facts…" Marie mumbles to herself.

"What's that?"

"Whitehead talks about the 'stubborn facts' that one resents, that one would like to ignore, but that are still a part of it all." Marie explains.

"You mean my bedroom?"

"Yes, that, too."

"Until recently it didn't bother me at all, I was happy with my bedroom; the way I see it you're the stubborn fact; apparently the whole system has to be expanded," Rudolf says, smiling to himself.

"So you think I'm the confounding element?" She grins up at him from below; she's about a foot shorter than him, the right height.

"You have to factor the facts into your thinking…"

"…says Whitehead!" Rudolf interrupts her.

"Yes, I know, I'm annoying, but I think about him twenty-four-seven." Marie is blushing.

"I've had a little look at what's being said about your Whitehead," Rudolf begins politely. "Well, the categorical scheme in *Process and Reality* is supposed to be really dark and incomprehensible and so abstract that you could just skip it altogether, and what the good man says about God seems to be reminiscent of mystic theology," he explains cautiously.

"Yes, he's too religious for scientists, too scientific

for theologians; everyone's having a tough time with him. The book started with a series of lectures, by the way…"

"And what exactly does he say in them?" Rudolf asks mischievously.

"*... So what exactly is infinitesimal calculus?*" she mimics him and pulls him around the fountain.

"No problem, it has to do with the analysis of limit values, infinitely tending to zero or something like that!" They both pause and laugh. Marie climbs onto the edge of the fountain, holds on to Rudolf's shoulders, clears her throat and playfully begins:

"Of course Whitehead's statements are abstract; he's a philosopher, and philosophy involves thought, but Whitehead in particular demands that abstraction be traced back to the concrete. Yes, philosophy has to account for how it is possible that thoughts, which are admittedly abstract but in which reality plays a part, can emerge from a concrete fact…"

Rudolf embraces her body, looks up at her with a grin. She grins back: "The world is in constant actuality: something is happening at every moment: in the most distant solar system and in the smallest atomic structure, in living organisms and in stones; we are part of these events that are constantly taking place…"

A school group approaches the fountain noisily, fifth- or sixth-graders. Three boys are balancing on the wall's edge, inside the pool the water is almost two feet deep.

"Get down!" yells the teacher.

The boys push each other from the edge, bellowing and chasing each other in circles. The rest of the class arrives slowly; the children stop in front of the high fountain, a gust of wind sends a spray of water in their direction; they scream and run towards the lake.

"...At the end of the day, the only justification for any thinking in Whitehead's terms is the clarification of immediate experience…" Marie continues and isn't distracted by the wind that turns and sprays water on her neck from behind:

"...Whitehead tries to include all of reality in the philosophical discussion with a new, adequate approach, and in addition to all of that, God has a place in it, too…"

"Beloved professor, I'd like to go and have a cup of coffee with you now," Rudolf says with a charming smile.

Marie lets herself slide down his chest and pauses, pressed firmly against him.

"See, you have your God and I have my infinity," he says happily. "Oh, how nice, Marie, we have so much time!"

They walk to the car briskly.

"When are you usually free?" Marie asks, "Wednesdays, Fridays, and Sundays are the best for me." She's starting to get cold.

"On Wednesdays I play squash with a friend, that's been a regular thing for us for years, Fridays I'm at my mother's, and Sunday is family day. We'll see," Rudolf says and takes her hand.

They pass the teahouse on their right, cross the long, grassy lawns, and come to the exit of the park. Rudolf holds the door of his light BMW open for her, Marie sits down on the passenger seat, buckles her seatbelt, he remains stooped down in the open door:

"You say Whitehead offers a new, adequate approach: Who wants to claim to know what kind of thinking is adequate?" he asks gloomily, stands up, slams the door shut, walks around the car, gets in, and starts driving towards Kiez.

13. *Bhagavad Gita*

It's early afternoon. Christian arrives and sits down next to me on the rattan sofa, has a coffee, our arms touch; he has a new, sweet smell, his jeans are new, too.

"I miss Johannes terribly…I could go pick him up later," he says.

"Johannes is at Elsa and Erich's today."

"Oh, damn it. He just watches TV when he's with them." Pause. Christian tries again.

"Remember when I told you about the Indian Jesuit priest Sebastian? He recently mentioned the Bhagavad Gita, I went and bought it immediately, but somehow I don't really understand the whole thing." He takes the book out of his coat, puts it on the table.

"So the warrior Arjuna is standing on the battlefield during combat, sees his relatives in the enemy's camp and is at his wits' end: should he really do his duty and fight against them, kill them? He'd rather run away, then he asks his merciful God for advice, but he's not impressed. Of course he has to act, says the merciful, but he has to act in a way that is also a non-action. And apart from that, a person's death is nothing to complain about, because what is, cannot *not* be, and what is not, cannot be, or something like that…"

"Maybe it's not the right reading material for you right now," I say vaguely.

"Yeah, yeah, I know, you don't take me seriously anyway."

There's no point in talking, but here we are again, so I take the well worn path of conversations we've had a hundred times before: "I can't consider whether I should act or not in the morning. I have a child whose rights demand that I get up whether I like it or not."

"Oh, I see, you have a child, well it just happens to be our son!" Christian's hands are trembling, he takes a sip of coffee.

"Do you know how much he misses you, Christian?"

"I just can't take it. I hate that man."

"Your hatred's taking all your energy. Remember what the doctor said?"

"Oh, give it a rest! There's no point!" Christian is glaring.

"...Talk to the Jesuit priest!"

"Nonsense! What's he going to do?" Christian

stands up, takes the book, pauses for a moment:

"The old man called yesterday."

"And?"

"I hung up. To hell with him!" Christian leaves. From where I am sitting, I watch him take his bike onto the sidewalk and disappear.

14. *African Violet*

It's already afternoon in the kitchen, I don't feel like doing anything, both legs ache; I put the left leg up and move my toes in little circles. Beyer Junior's blue Audi pulls into the courtyard. It takes a long time for mother and son to walk over from the parking lot. Mrs. Beyer is leaning on her son's arm; her hat has shifted, sharp wrinkles drawn through her face. Her son is speaking to her insistently, puts his arm around her. They slowly approach the front door.

It's getting dark. I light the candle at the little wooden cross on the side table; the glow of the flame melts into the black cachepot with the dark blue-purple African violet. My gaze lingers on Christ on the cross…

- You, the Son of Man from Galilee…Not a god in eternal distance, you want to be a god in eternal proximity; you descended from the heavens, became flesh; you want to be part of our lowliness and let us take part in your heavenliness. Out of love… I can't really believe what you are saying, but do I have to? Isn't it enough that it has been said? The man's eternal longing for the truly good, beautiful, and just. What you proclaim exceeds everything else. Even Plato didn't think about that; still looking for perfection in the square and any proportion of it in the golden ratio; but he had to have suspected something because he presumed: If there were ever anyone like you, he would be castigated, tortured, and crucified… Would he have recognized you?

The phone rings.

"Matthias!"

"Mrs. Michaelis, I wanted to ask when you have office hours so I can come and see you about my term paper."

"Thursday next week, 2 p.m.!" I respond promptly; I had already scheduled it.

"Great, thank you, that works."

But it seemed there was more. I give him a moment, hear his breath.

"Do you think I could include Spinoza's *amor Dei intellectualis*?" he asks timidly.

I feel a glow inside my chest; I see the young man's sincere face, his reddish hair, his sparkling eyes that seem to be able to take in the whole world.

"Yes, of course… Intellectual cognition that seizes the whole body and effects love: that's a wonderful thought…" I pause, feeling my own excitement rise: "...From there you could also take a look at Whitehead, who by means of concretization carefully examines every state of being affected; body and mind ultimately meeting in one truth. We can talk about it on Thursday."

"Thank you, get well soon, Mrs. Michaelis!"

"Thanks, Matthias!"

It's past 5 p.m. I was going to get primroses. But since Johannes is coming home later he won't be able to see them anyway.

Heavy faintness comes over me; I take a sip of water, lean my head against the wall, the crucifix that just reaches the side of the cachepot in my line of vision.

I long for Anne's soft voice.

15. *The Neighbor*

The door bell rings, I startle, Mrs. Beyer's son, could he have a quick chat with me? We sit down in the kitchen.

"You have a nice place here, a proper eat-in kitchen!" he says; his apartment in Cologne has a big kitchen, too.

"You're moving to Cologne?"

"Yes, I just got engaged!" He gives a forced laugh. "My bride-to-be is from Cologne, we're getting married in a month."

"Congratulations."

"Yeah, yeah, but my mother…She's afraid that I'm leaving her, and then there were today's test results at the doctor." He hesitates for a moment. "She has cancer, bowel cancer. Unfortunately I have to leave for Cologne really early tomorrow morning, but my sister is coming to take care of her. In case my mother doesn't hear the bell, could my sister pick up the key at here at your place, around nine? I don't have time to go to Rudow today." Young Mr. Breyer looks pale.

"Don't worry about it, I'll be here."

He thanks me and disappears into the elevator.

I have not had a decent meal today, fry a few eggs, cut some tomatoes. The pizzeria is almost empty. The waiters and kitchen staff are sitting together and eating. The next rush will start soon.

A black limousine turns into the street, slowly pulls up, stops in the middle of the lane, the driver looks up in my direction; during the day you can't see me from down there, we tried, it looks like Christian's father, the face staring up – no, cannot be him, Hagemann lives abroad, this car has a German license plate. Two cars honk. The black car starts moving. And what if it is Paul? Could be a rental car. I wolf down the eggs and tomatoes, a slice of brown bread with it.

The candle smokes terribly; I put it out, cut the wick short. Mrs. Breyer's son leaves the house towards the courtyard. I feel cold, get a blanket from the back room, see Mrs. Breyer standing on the balcony above the ramp that leads to the underground parking lot; she waves goodbye to her son, waves and waves; he waves back, gets into the car, pulls out, and turns to the right, looks back once more, signals with his flasher, and off he goes. Mrs. Beyer walks back into her apartment, closes the curtains.

Slowly the other tenants arrive. I go back to sitting in the kitchen, put the blanket over my legs.

16. *Bad Dreams*

Marie and Rudolf are standing in the no waiting zone, in front of the Café Ecke Knobelsdorffer. She is lying across the gear shift, both arms snuggled around Rudolf's neck, his hands busy with her breasts, erect pleasure for a good while.

"*The mercy of erection*, that is so true, something a woman just can't understand," Rudolf says in a husky voice. At the end of the street a garbage truck appears. He takes his hands out of her sweater. "At night I often dream about an old Greek man. I can't figure out what this character means. Do you know anything about dreams?"

"No. Have you been to Greece many times?"

"Twice, but I don't see the connection." Rudolf looks out of the window. "This dream always awakens feelings of guilt inside me, you know, I don't feel very good, sometimes I think I'm sick."

"But you're very healthy, apart from your back."

Marie smiles and puts her head on his chest. They can hear the garbage truck coming closer. "Probably some kind of father figure," she says offhandedly.

"No, no, I've definitely got my father out of my system, I'm sure of that; it's got to be something else..." Rudolf puts his hands on the steering wheel, drums his fingers nervously. "Can you come over to my place tonight?" he asks in a husky voice.

Johannes could sleep at Christian's or Auntie's, Marie considers quickly, or with the twins, no, not the twins, Johannes had said that the twins' mama screams at night, so best at Christian's...

"Yes, around 9 p.m.," she says.

The big truck is already roaring behind them. Rudolf starts the car, puts it into gear, and they take off.

17. *Strange Visit*

It got dark. The workmen upstairs are gone. I turn on the light, lower the blinds, rotate the slats. Lit up windows in the nearby houses, like an advent calendar.

"Mamamamamamamama...!" Johannes has seen me, his clear, chattering voice rises up to me. The three of them come running, the little one with arms stretched between Elsa and Erich; he lets himself fall to his knees with a giggle: one, two, three, whee! The old folks start running, lift him up, let him fly over the asphalt for a few meters, he stands again. I open the window.

"Again!" Johannes begs, hanging between the two.

"No, enough." Erich is gasping for air.

"This one's ready for bed," Elsa calls out to me.

"No way!" Johannes protests.

"It got late, we had to watch *Hart to Hart* with him. Don't worry, it's a harmless show! By the way,

Günther wanted to speak to you, something happened in kindergarten today!"

Johannes lets himself fall into Erich's arms with a giggle.

"So, that's enough," Erna says resolutely and takes the little one's hand.

Johannes and I take the elevator up. He throws himself on the bed with his clothes, "I am sooo tired..." and remains lying with his eyes closed, first pointing one, then the other foot towards me while I take off his shoes and socks.

"Mama, Nadja's sister is going to be baptized, they're going to have a big party. What is baptized?"

"Being baptized means becoming a child of god."

"Am I a child of god?" Now his eyes are open.

"Yes, of course."

"So I've been baptized, too?"

"No, Papa and I wanted to wait until you were able to decide that for yourself." I help him out of his pants and sweater.

"Was Papa baptized?"

"Yes."

"Were you baptized, Mama?"

"Yes."

"Right, now quickly go and brush your teeth!"

"I want to be baptized, too," Johannes says, puts on

his pajamas, trots briefly into the bathroom, then to bed. "Nadja has to go to the hairdresser, she's going to get curls and a white dress, like an angel, Nadja says," he murmurs, turns, takes his teddy bear, and falls asleep immediately; I tuck him in, turn off the light, and decide to speak to the parish minister soon.

Johannes's backpack is lying on the floor. In the half-opened side pocket are three shriveled chestnuts, a candy wrapper, and a colorful invitation to the carnival, everything covered in sand; I take everything out, pour out the sand, put my hand into the corners of the bag, and suddenly have cigarette ends and matches between my fingers, tremor in my heart, how did they get into the backpack? Has Johannes been smoking? What happened in kindergarten today? Call Günther! No, he asked the parents to understand that he didn't want to give out his private number. Wait until tomorrow.

I go to the kitchen, mechanically put away the dishes, turn off the light, rotate the blinds horizontally, sit down on the rattan couch, both legs up. The apartment that had the photo shoot this afternoon is dark, the Italian restaurant in full swing.

- On Sunday I will take Johannes to the playground or to the movies; I will clean his room with him…

I have to talk to someone. Should I try Irene again?

And what if junior picks up, or even worse, Klaus, just back from the States? No!

It's 8 p.m., time for the evening news. Silly really, not to have a television; after all it would be nice to learn a few things that are going on in the world.

Call Rudolf after all? I have my hand on the receiver; his number is stored in my brain.

..."A love that doesn't grow dies," was one of his final sentences, bitterly negating what they had already experienced. He blamed himself entirely for the unhappy ending of their short relationship; he was evidently unable to love; admittedly he felt love inside him but this love somehow couldn't radiate outward, and in general the power to love was really quite rare, he had read that in Camus, and apparently he, Rudolf, belonged to the majority of mankind.

"Maybe I'm gay!" he defiantly declared at one point, referring to his dream with the Greek, in any case his friend had advised him to look into it seriously.

One midmorning at the end of April, the day finally came: They met in the café on Steubenplatz, he had called shortly before.

Marie was excited to see him so spontaneously, cancelled a doctor's appointment, and rushed to the café. He held her hand the whole time, they talked about this and that, he got increasingly quiet. Suddenly he said that this was their last meeting and started his litany: He did not want to continue to drag her down into the vortex of his negativity, did not want to infect her with it, the demarcation between the light and dark elements had to be upheld; her perspective was just different from his; where she saw catharsis, his eyes saw only arthritis; where he could at best discover grey, she would fill the world with color; next to her he felt like a scorching desert that was drying everything up and would only hurt her…

Marie's insides froze, she felt her body shrink to an unlivable minimum.

"I would rather be unhappy with you than happy without you," she utters her pathetic truth.

"No, Marie; I had such high hopes, but it just won't work!"

"Why not? Another woman?"

"That would be easy. No, I don't know myself. It just won't work, you have to accept that." He had cut the threads. He paid, they left, he to his BMW, she to her Deux-Cheveaux, and they both surrendered to the same flow of traffic, with considerable distance between them.

"Really? It didn't work in bed?" Irene said hours later as Marie was sitting in front of her, sobbing hysterically.

"He just wasn't the one," Anne tried to comfort her distraught friend on the phone.

The downstairs doorbell rings. At this hour?

"Who is it?"

Street noise, the intercom crackles.

"Paul, Hagemann..."

My heart is racing, I push the buzzer to let him in. The last time I saw Paul was at his wife's funeral. It takes a while for the old man to arrive upstairs, he doesn't know the apartment, knows only that it's on the third floor. I wait in the doorway, the elevator opens, Paul Hagemann appears: tall, elegant, tanned, his head tilted slightly, he slowly comes towards me.

"Good evening, Marie, I'm sorry for dropping in like this…"

I lead him to the kitchen, turn on the light. He sits down on a chair, looks around.

"You work here?"

"I had an operation on my veins, am on sick leave at the moment so I've set up a kind of headquarters here, it's really handy."

For a moment the doctor in him comes alive, he asks for details. I talk about the bandage that had been wrapped too tightly and the blue spots on my foot. He interrupts me:

"Can I see Johannes?"

"Yes, but he's already asleep." I lead him into the child's room, the glow of the hallway lamp falls across the child's bed, I leave him alone with his grandchild. Then Paul comes back into the kitchen, puts an envelope on the table:

"For the little one, and if needed, my address in Spain…"

"You live in Majorca?"

"Yes, for some time; adios, Marie!" He leaves.

"Adios, Paul!"

I turn the light off, put on Satie's early piano works, one of Rudolf's records, sink onto the bed, points, lines, circles roll around in spirals before my eyelids, locks open, pain floods through all organs.

> …Rudolf in his dark red-green striped bathrobe welcomes her at the door, his whole apartment

is pregnant with spruce needles, eucalyptus, and Satie's strangely layered harmonies. He leads her into the steaming bathroom, climbs into the tub, slender, well-toned with a nicely padded bottom, and disappears into the foaming greenish water. He leads her into the bedroom, the scent of health emanating from his pores. The bed was made recently, the blanket pulled back, the bedside lamp glows softly.

He pulls her low-cut sweater over her shoulders, searches for her lips, strips her, penetrates her, starts pounding, thoroughly, almost angrily, the bed creaks, they let themselves fall on the floor, interlocked, biting until there's blood, her lust remains untouched even though they haven't skipped anything, the skin on her back is scraped, face is puffy, two hours of sleep, the next day again and so on, the little one alone at night for the first time, she feels wasted, broken, wretched.

"Maybe we're not a good fit after all," she blurts out one morning when he enquires on the phone whether she has made it back home alright.

"Thanks, I just wanted to get that confirmed."

No, she didn't mean it like that. He hangs up…

The record is over, piercing headache, I take an aspirin, lie down again, I'm cold. I crawl under the blanket, shreds of dreams: Rudolf stands in front of a red brick building in blue coveralls; he's dragging a bag of bones; a shoe rack falls next to him, shoes everywhere; Johannes is playing tag on a high wall with the twins; they laugh, squeal, try to push each other off; the floor is made of stone; I'm scared.

18. *With Her Hat On*

A heavy thud. I wake with a start, Johannes! I rush into his room, he's asleep. I must have been dreaming, lie down again, my heart is pounding, just before 6 a.m., I get up, go into the kitchen, turn on the light, dim it low, turn on the coffee machine, I feel sick. I take a sip of water. A fire siren wails briefly. Then silence again. The coffee machine splutters. Sudden flashes of emergency lights on the hallway ceiling, I go into the backroom, Mrs. Breyer's balcony door is open, a chair at the balcony railing, on the sloping ground a dressed body, hat and bag nearby; the caretaker and his wife stand in the courtyard, the young woman is sobbing; dark figures in the windows; an emergency physician and paramedics are occupied with the broken body, put it on a stretcher, slide it into the car, drive away.

"She jumped with her hat on!" the caretaker says loudly.

I walk back into the kitchen, sit down on the rattan couch, shaking all over and trying to calm my breathing.

Anne

Heat of Summer

1. *Timbres*

It's night; there is a suffocating heat in the room. Anne sits in front of the music stand with her back exposed, the violin on her knees. She gave the new Bach bow a try; finally the chords of the Chaconne sound like Bach composed them, all four parts at once, without arpeggio, like a soft organ-sound, the whole Solo-Partita a flowing prayer.

She must have been sitting there like that for a while, her eyes and ears hurt even though the room is pleasantly lit and quiet; Anne gets up, puts the violin in its case, clips the bow onto the inside of the lid, lays the dark green and golden embroidered velvet blanket over the honey-colored instrument, latches the clasps on the side, sets the scores in the cupboard.

Outside summer is raging, permeates the wide-open windows and doors, seeps through walls and skin. Anne walks onto the deck. The surrounding houses are dark, no one around, husband and son not there either: Julian had to go to New York last week, an inheritance, an uncle had died, and Pablo insisted on spending his vacations with friends in Malta this year.

Longing for the South. She was lucky and just managed to get on a flight to Palma. One week in Mallorca, alone for the first time after so many years!

Anne walks back into the study, looks through her old records for Weber's timbre compositions; she loves Weber's subtle nuances of the instruments' vibrations, has not listened to him for a while, chooses his orchestral transcription of the Ricercata from the Musical Offering by Bach, lies down on the deck chair outside. Warm darkness envelops her, stars and the firmament fall over her, the sounds of the individual instruments blend together gently and drift toward her: the muffled trombone, horn and trumpet, soft harp, flute, clarinet, and oboe mysteriously iridescent in pianissimo, breaking up Bach's fugue theme, more and more instruments join, condense into a single flow of sounds, carrying the whole fugue away with them, swelling into a sea of sounds, melt, wither.

Anne drifts off into a dreamless sleep.

2. *Wild Roses*

The cabin door is being locked. The metal colossus starts moving, rolls leisurely to the runway. The perfectly tanned stewardess demonstrates with a smile where to pull when the life vest has to be inflated; as soon as the battery comes into contact with water, a light will come on automatically.

Anne leans her head back. The exhaustion runs deep: the move to the bigger apartment, weeks of this heat over Berlin with high levels of ozone, orchestra rehearsals up till the very end, and all afternoon yesterday in the muggy city. In the evening she had met Marie and given her the keys so she could water the plants. "Come back in one piece!" she called after Anne.

The machine is still. Finally the stewardesses sit down. Waiting for clearance for take-off. Anne closes her eyes. How often she used to commute back and forward between Berlin and Palma. All of it so long ago, the memory like someone else's story, yet it is she that experienced all of this; the past is stored in her body, engraved in the alleys, the mountains, the sea there.

Now the full power of the engines. Anne is not afraid. Being at the mercy of the pilots' experience and the perfection of the machine is calming to her. She is not responsible for anything here. Tegel and surroundings lie tilted in the round window, they're climbing. In those crucial seconds until the no smoking sign vanishes Anne prays involuntarily.

- Lord Jesus Christ, have mercy on me.

This ancient formula, thousands of years old, buried somewhere inside her, comes up of its own accord. The tremendous cry for the mercy of a god effects something like love for all creatures and for herself inside her, sorrows and fears vanish, and what remains is an essence of gratitude, gratitude to have been able to live.

They fly over a thin blanket of clouds, illuminated from above like in a theater, with dull shreds of landscape below. Anne surrenders to the drone of the engines. Her body relaxes perceptibly, a strange blend of consciousness and feeling, Emilio is suddenly very near, tatters of memories drift past: Barcelona – her first concert tour – meeting Emilio in the Café de l'Opéra– love at first sight – the child midway through her studies at the university – marriage and relocation to Pollensa, Emilio's Majorcan home – the sudden end…

A woman sits down in Anne's row, in the aisle seat.

"My husband's smoking. I can't stand it back there," says the woman. She has red blemishes on her neck, on her blouse wild roses arch against a white background.

"I'm already totally woozy. I got really nauseous so I went to ask the stewardess and she said I could come and sit up here. I'm jealous, you here all on your own! Be thankful you're here without a man. I'd rather have five children than one man!"

The woman leans over to Anne:

"You aren't married, are you?"

"I am."

"Well, I wouldn't have thought. So young and attractive, so, how shall I say it, emancipated; you don't have to be these days…" The woman is looking for the end of the seatbelt. "I just told him I'm going to the toilet. Let him deal with it." She fastens the seatbelt. "Have you been married for a while, I mean, always to the same man?" the woman continues, shifting around in her seat until she is finally comfortable.

"No." Was this her first trip to Majorca, Anne asks her back.

"No, no, we've gone to Majorca every year! For twenty-five years. We have an apartment there, you know, in Alcudia. It was cheap back then; we used to vacation in Ca'n Picafort and one day…"

Rather than listening to the apartment story, Anne wants to hear more about the husband problem:

"Have you never thought about divorce?"

The smiling stewardess hands out the packaged lunches.

"Oh, I've hemmed and hawed about it hundreds of times, it's not so easy… You know what it's like…"

A second stewardess brings the beverages.

"Tea or coffee?"

"Tea, please."

"I'd like a coffee," says the woman. "My girlfriends always say, 'Oh, your husband, gosh, he's nice!' Because none of them have one and they envy me of course. You know: 'A man's a man, even if he sits in bed and coughs!' When he's with me he acts like he's terminally ill, doesn't say a word, puffs away, and as soon as the hags come to visit he turns on the charm, every time I feel like I could just kill him!" The woman is now occupied with the cold cuts and doesn't seem to want to talk anymore. Anne doesn't encourage her, sips the hot tea, takes her time. The quark tastes excellent, the butter is hard but fresh; she puts it in little slices on the chilled bread.

"Every love dies down eventually, as strong as it may be," the woman begins again. "After a few years everything's old hat. Or can you imagine Romeo and Juliet married, with children? Nope, old Shakespeare knew, preferred to have them die straightaway… ha ha ha!" The woman gets up, takes the opened lunch package, says she's feeling better and wants to go see how her husband is doing.

"Goodbye!

"Goodbye," Anne calls after her and starts to doze.

The flight goes by quickly; she orders an orange juice over the Alps and eagerly awaits Marseille, where the sea stretches out like a giant metal-blue washboard. Then finally, the outline of the large island! The bold coastal range cuts a sharp line into the sea, auburn acres of soil extend like tennis courts across the land. The old wind mills can be seen during the landing, some turning lazily as if they had been forgotten. Gentle landing, the passengers applaud. Palma de Mallorca!

Her seatbelt remains fastened even though Anne wants to start running into the southern splendor! Everything at the airport runs smoothly despite it being the height of the season. At the baggage claim

Anne sees the wild roses, then the woman.

"So what did your husband say about you being away for so long?"

"Oh, he was sleeping, he didn't even notice." The woman sulkily points at a tall man in his seventies, who, leaning on a pale walking cane, looks through the crowd disinterestedly.

"That's him, that's my husband." Pride resonates in her voice.

"Well then, have a nice vacation!" Anne hurries to the exit.

3. *Mother Hulda*

"Aquí, Scñora!"

A taxi driver, unusually eager by Majorcan standards, holds the car door open for Anne, takes care of her suitcase.

"Graçis, al Port de Pollença!"

The driver is visibly delighted by her Mallorquin and the fact that she knows Pollensa, that he can tell her about the heat these last few weeks and about his background in Pollensa. The people of Pollensa are proud of their town, and justifiably so; even the history books call this ancient Roman village the ultimate beautiful, holy town. Nestled in fertile, rolling landscapes, surrounded by gardens and fincas, framed by the massive, rocky mountain Puig de Maria with its cloister and the softly rising Calvario, the rose-colored mountain range behind it and the sea within sight, Pollensa also has seven wonderful churches.

"...And the big music festival every summer with

international artists! Yes: New York – Paris – London –Pollensa!" the taxi driver exclaims enthusiastically and shifts into fifth gear, on the freeway headed toward Alcudia.

Anne doesn't want to hear any more, doesn't want to have to speak any more; he'll stop at some point, after all the Mallorquin value discretion. She opens the window, only heat drifts in, she takes shallow breaths, everything is tantalizing, the air pressure, the proximity of the sea, the high sky, the sounds, even the exhaust fumes smell of the South, promise adventure.

Unbelievable. Everything is still there: Almond and fig trees, olive groves surrounded by high cypresses. A black chicken strides over the auburn soil under orange trees. A lemon tree lets its branches hang low, to allow its fruit to be plucked like at Mother Hulda's? Past the turnoff to Pollensa, plane trees line the side of the street, to the right a wide, fertile plain sprawls out, to the left the mountains beckon mysteriously. Anne's heart is throbbing, her blood is being driven by her joy, rushing to her temples, lust seizes her, irrepressible lust for this part of the world. She snuggles into her seat; Julian called her yesterday morning, his voice sounding dry and hoarse:

"I miss you! New York is as hot as a frying pan, the

heirs are infuriating, they're all idiots, but Dr. Smith seems to be able to hold his ground...Say hello the harbor for me! Take care!"

And the ocean lies between them again.

4. *El Calvario*

Puerto de Pollensa! Anne loves her little hotel room with mountain view where she bumps into the opened windows when she wants to go past the bed to the mirror, where she needs to be careful to keep one of the persianas closed so that the neighbors on the corner cannot see her, an elderly gay couple who themselves do not want to be seen. There is an arbitrary messiness in her room with an order that only she understands; everything is somehow in its place, for this week at least, in this heat.

The mountains are at the foot of her bed, the uninterrupted sky above them promises mysterious joy, sea and beach are waiting, she has everything at her disposal, she is filled with a sense of lightness, the feeling of freedom, a freedom that is close to chaos. She wants to be everywhere at once, her senses are eagerly opened to the Mediterranean spectacle; eyes, ears, nose, mouth, lungs, skin soak up the blue of the sky, the turquoise of the sea, the pink-silver mountains, the velvet air, the hot sand and stones, the muddled scents and sounds during the day and night.

She rents a bicycle, rides out on the big jetty past the glossy yachts and boats to the lighthouse far out at sea, enjoys the Coca, dripping in olive oil and garnished with fried eggplant and peppers in the shadow of the little tower, in no time she is back on the quiet stone plateaus at the pine beach where Pablo learned to walk; she strolls along the water, through children splashing and building sandcastles, walks up the promenade to the Casinet, sits down in the front garden, orders coffee and water; young people at the bar, soul music in the background, all around her lavish summery hustle and bustle; waves, vibrations of all kinds penetrate her, engulf her, carry her away into the vibrating vastness of the bay to the dancing sails out there between heaven and sea. Something suddenly brushes her neck, anxiety seizes her, her heart tenses, she gets up, takes the bus to Pollensa, seven kilometers into the heart of the country, climbs the 365 steps of the Calvary, past the sacred beauty of the cypresses, to the chapel all the way at the top, sits down on the small wall on the hillside; in front of her the north coast: Cala San Vicente peeks out from between deep blue mountain ranges, the bay of

Pollensa lies next to it like a lake; in the misty distance the church of Alcudia floats like a cathedral… Anne sinks into the horizon, her body expands, dissolves into the vastness, and she feels the undivided sky above her as it melts into the mist of the sea, with the scent of dried grasses, the vibration of the hot stones, the whispers of dancing insects, heaven all around her.

She used to come up here with Emilio every day, in the summer, at night, too, when the stars were dripping and Ursa Major stood just above the tip of the roof of the chapel, almost touching the little cross of the church.

Anne cannot bear the beauty, runs down the holy steps barefoot with her insides pulsating wildly. Suddenly a heavy peal of bells from the ashlar-shaped tower of the *Parroquia*, she continues slowly. Halfway up the mountain is Isabel and Juan's house, for sale.

She used to sit here with Isabel and the children, Pablo still on all fours. Anne squats on the warm steps, her feet pointed toward medieval Pollensa. The late sun pours gold over the ochre of the intricate roofs and walls; behind the high, dark cypresses the valley is glowing bluish-green and flower meadows are shining, a bit like a Gauguin, somewhere white linens are hanging.

They came from Valencia – Isabel, Juan, and the five daughters; life here was healthier, house and garden affordable. Juan was a painter, too, Emilio admired his older friend, whose art was so different from his own. Juan painted like one possessed, had to sell the paintings before he could really finish them. The money was never enough. He set up a chicken farm that generated some additional income and gave them fresh eggs every day. The girls needed warm clothes, the youngest one was just two, coughed constantly and just too thin.

One wet and cold winter evening, Anne arrives to see the children standing in front of Isabel with their mouths open wide, Isabel pouring a big spoonful of a thick, white liquid for each of them.

"Calcium with vitamins, that's what they need now," Isabel explains, unfazed by the girls' contorted faces as they swallow the paste bravely. Isabel looks tired, her strawberry blond, naturally curly hair hangs over her puffy face like a wig; she is only twenty-nine but child birth and hardship have exhausted her prematurely.

"I also studied art in Valencia, then had the children, my mother used to help out, now she's got her own problems; Juan's trying but it's just not enough. His parents had something against our relationship right from the start, I guess I'm just not refined enough for them, well, we had to marry without them; I don't think they even know that they have grandchildren."

Two tourists come up the steps slowly, one carrying a camera on his shoulder, stopping every once in a while, filming the paradise that lies before him, followed by a black and white spotted dog with short legs that trots along behind as if he belonged there.

Sometimes the two friends went out into the landscape to paint; Emilio had a hasty way of painting, painted almost angrily, as if he wanted to force the overwhelming abundance around him onto the canvas, and yet he was almost always disappointed with what he carried home. Juan preferred to paint in the studio, he only made sketches outside; he applied the paints in the style of the Old Masters which took a lot of time but gave his paintings a special depth and luminosity.

"Juan takes way too much time to make a painting; he should paint like Emilio," Isabel says one night over dinner. Juan leaves the table silently, goes over to the children on the terrace. Emilio defends his friend:

"Your husband really is an extraordinary artist, Isabel. His technique just doesn't allow him to paint more quickly."

"But he can't afford to do that, he has a wife and five children!" retorts Isabel. Blood surges to her cheeks. "You and your art! Just leave me alone!" she shouts angrily and leaves the house.

Juan slowly returns with the little one on his arm, stops in front of his friends, eyes downcast:

"I'm sorry; Isabel isn't happy, it's all very hard for her." He hesitates. "We learned yesterday that she's pregnant again. I don't know what to do, I have to leave now, too, thanks for everything, let's go, kids!"

The girls hug little Pablo, say goodbye to Anne and Emilio, and follow their father. From that day on Isabel rarely went into town, her growing body became apparent under her wide dresses.

Anne looks through the keyhole into the dark hall, at the back, to the left, the window to the patio, tatters of curtains on both sides, to the right the wooden bench at the wall. A cat snuggles between Anne's legs, purrs like mad. "I don't have anything!" Anne says but the animal, its fur thick and glossy, doesn't really want anything else.

One evening Juan is suddenly standing before Anne and Emilio. Pale, shaking all over, he weeps bitterly; Isabel had given birth to a baby girl, it was dead, he panted. "The doctor said it was a still birth, the doctor has issued a death certificate, it was a still birth!" he repeats again and again, horrified, as if his wife had suffocated the child…

When everything was over, Isabel took her five daughters and went back to Valencia; Juan stayed behind in Pollensa, painting obsessively again and sending everything he could spare to his wife and children.

The bells have fallen silent. The sun has disappeared behind the mountains. Anne descends the final part of the Calvarios, past the shoemaker's fat wife, walks through the lanes with the familiar smell of *Vajillas* and garlic fried in olive oil, stops in front of Emilio's parents' abandoned house. The green of the window sills has crumbled, the wooden strips weathered.

- No, she hadn't been able to help the two old folks at the time. Onward. She walks past the church walls, the side portal is open, she pulls her cap down farther over her forehead, enters the huge ship, the sacristan is busy dousing the candles, a sea of flowers in the sanctuary, in the first side altar to the left Christ hangs high above on the cross, life-sized, arms stretched out as if he wanted to hug the whole world, his face tilted towards his chest, a golden crown of thorns on his head. There he is, waiting. God's endless patience. Anne kneels down in front of the beautiful figure, masked, indiscriminate; the sacristan wants to close up, she has to leave.

Outside the sky has turned black. At the end of the small lane lies the brightly lit market place, nicely dressed children are running around, beautiful people are strolling about, parents are sitting judiciously in groups at big tables, the older people chatter and fan themselves to cool down, like always.

The Bar Espanyol is showing the soccer world cup. Anne sits down at the back wall, orders some water, and enjoys her anonymity; nobody really seems to notice her.

First half. The Brazilians are playing wonderfully, nevertheless it’s still 0:0, general disappointment. The little waiter smiles at her, Anne gets up, pays, and leaves, hurries across the market place through the screaming children, down the steps to the taxi stand.

At the harbor she is welcomed by the garland of lights along the bay, the sea of lights on the firmament. She lies down on the hot stones of a jetty, dizziness seizes her, happiness and pain are equally rampant inside her, she closes her eyes, surrenders to the lapping of the waves, the muted laughs of a couple somewhere, the song of the crickets and distant dance music. One of those enchanted Mediterranean nights.

When she gets back to the hotel it’s 1:0 in the Brazilians’ favor. General jubilation.

5. *Object Immortality*

During the day she yearns for the sea. She sinks into the yielding mass, waves enfold every vibration of her body, holding her in a soft embrace; it is with pleasure that she surrenders to the salty element, letting herself sink up to the roots of her hair, floating like a jellyfish with tentacles, like seaweed, weightless, submissive, the boundary between her and the sea is no longer detectable, wonderful expanse, relinquishing, falling, dissolving, vanishing; suddenly dizziness, fear, heart palpitations, breathlessness, she hurries back, lies exhausted on the shallow shore, waves full of sand coursing through her hair, flowing around her limbs, washing over her, sky and sun circle behind closed lids, to lie here forever, to vanish, to be buried, to become one with the sand for eternity, dead. Why is she concerned with her own death? It would almost be satisfying in that she wouldn't be able to add anything more to her existence; her body would dissolve into elements that would regroup, begin a new process, merge into a new state, enjoying objective immortality, so to speak. One could only hope that, in this process of dissolution, it was not irrelevant that the cells in question were hers, and furthermore, that a tender and caring god would ensure that, in the course of all this, none of them would be lost. Not a comforting thought. But was there any comfort to be had? In any case, her death would mean losing everything that existed, the loss of actuality, reality. Inconceivable, grim, as reality encompassed everything she loved, everything that was of value to her; reality was the precious date that pervaded her constantly, creating her perceptions and connecting her to the world. And her perceptions were what they were so that she could be what she was. Yes, she loved reality.

"Do you believe in the resurrection of the dead?" she asked Emilio after Sunday mass, the market in front of the church was still in full swing, they had been invited to lunch with the parents, Pablo running between them.

"I believe in the resurrection of the Lord," Emilio responded calmly.

"But what does that mean?" Emilio remained silent. "Is that some kind of magic incantation that you recite every Sunday?" she asked impatiently. Emilio's simple way of talking about religious matters irritated her; he was usually such a critical person.

"I sense truth in it," Emilio said softly and put his arm around her.

What truth, in the face of the despair that his sudden death left behind? No, time does not heal all wounds; something in her had died with Emilio. His mother followed him shortly afterwards, her heart broken, and his father wandered through town for days, his powers of comprehension gone; his memory shattered; they brought him to the Residencia where he lived for a little while longer, without any memories whatsoever.

Anne's parents finally came and took her and little Pablo back to Berlin.

6. *Congealing Time*

Enough. Salt traces are forming on her skin, the sun is burning red spots through the crystals. She gets up, plunges headfirst into the water again, takes a few strong breast and back strokes, breathes deeply; the balance has been restored. Life envelops her, graspable, she wants to savor it, wants to take more pleasure in it, wants to ride her bike into the heart of the country where it is lonely and silent, wants to be captured by the blaze of the summer, wants to go to the Cala to drink a Cortado, right at the sea, in the little café, under the tamarisks, on the terrace, at the open sea. To Cala San Vicente!

She puts on the short, strapless dress over her wet bathing suit, puts on strong sun screen, dons sunglasses and a visor, packs her towel, bag, and sandals into the bike basket and rides towards the town exit.

It is about 4 p.m., a significant distance with a steady incline lies ahead of her; just outside of Pollensa at the three long, arid palm trees the route turns to the right towards the Cala, a road that corkscrews through pastures and fields, alongside the dried-up riverbed; then after a final ascent there is a hill with a view of the expanse of sea lying far below, perpendicular to the sky.

Anne is looking forward to the ride, the caressing of the velvet air, the shimmer, the chirping of the heat and the creatures, looking forward to feeling her tendons, muscles, her heart, her lungs in exertion; more than anything she enjoys the arbitrariness of her undertaking and passes the last houses at the harbor with an elated sense of freedom and a little defiance, against whomever or whatever.

The route lies straight ahead. On the other end, Pollensa hovers and oscillates over the steaming asphalt like a mirage in milky-white fog. The air is anything but velvet, rather aggressively hot and Anne's movements do not cool her at all, instead they have the effect of a fan and oven that just propel the heat toward her body more intensely.

- A breeze will come from somewhere, she thinks fleetingly and pedals rhythmically, feeling the equally rhythmical pulsating of her blood. She is alone on the usually heavily trafficked Carretera, the most important road connecting Puerto de Pollensa,

Pollensa, and Palma. There is not a soul in sight; the usual tanned tourists on bikes who continue from their beachside sunbathing into the countryside are nowhere to be seen. The heat slows her down. Anne hardly makes any progress. A cabriolet speeds past her, the top closed. The driver looks at her strangely. She concentrates on her breathing and the movement of her pedaling, struggles ahead one meter at a time. High rock walls protrude into the lane, the glow that has been stored in them rolls towards her even more relentlessly; the bathing suit has dried on her body; heart and breath faster now, the movements slower, she creeps, wants to turn back, no, too late, to the right, farther along the blistering rocks, her pulse is hammering, her face feels scarlet red, the asphalt is boiling, there's no one anywhere, just don't stop…

> … Time is slipping away, eternity, night without firmament; she floats through the streets, crowds of people, is met with astonished looks, is she ok? Dark windows everywhere. Longing tears inside her, longing for existence, for life, bittersweet formulas for something lost, irretrievable. She floats through the city center, to stop off somewhere, no, not just anywhere, there, a bar with colorful

lights, snatches of flamenco, laughter, a babble of voices, the clinking of glasses and dishes, suffocating cigarette smoke, sweat, coffee, wine. Curious eyes glance at her. Dizziness seizes her, Emilio lies in repose in between glasses, bottles, and fragrant plants, hands folded at chest height on a gold-embroidered blanket, without the shape of a body. The coffin lid is being slammed shut. She rushes towards it, screaming:

- No!

Nobody notices her. A choir drowns out her cry…

- *Santa Maria, Madre de Deus, ruega por nosotros pecadores...*

- No!

Nobody hears her,

- *...ahora y en la hora de nuestra muerte, Jesus...*

Crowds of people file past her. The lights go out. The choir falls silent. She is standing outside, alone. The bar is closed. Emilio appears next to her.

- Emilio! You're alive?

He does not respond.

- What is living, Emilio?

Emilio keeps silent.

- How do the others do it?

- They pretend to know it, she hears Emilio whisper.

- And us?

- We have each other, that's living.

Now it is Julian's voice. Julian is very close. His words fall into her soothingly. Where it had just been dark, there is light now. Her whole system is flooded by love, it gets brighter and brighter inside her, around her…

Strangers standing over her. What do they want from her? Where is Julian?

"The name of your hotel," someone is trying to get her to speak. "Do you speak English?"

What's happening? Her body trails after her, she feels cold and sick. It goes dark again.

7. *The Physicist*

When Anne opens her eyes, she is looking at a closed window. The darkly tinted panes let only a dim light into the tiny room. It is pleasantly cool, but the noise of the air conditioner makes her nervous. She is lying on a small bed; next to her hand, a bell. She is thirsty and she wants the window to be opened. She rings the bell. A nurse enters.

"Please open the window!"

"No, Señora, it is still too hot!"

"Where am I?"

"In the Ambulancia. Luckily they found you in time, a German... "

Anne doesn't want to know who found her. She just wants the window to be opened and something to drink. The nurse hands her a glass of water.

Anne's body seems to have rooted into the mattress. She looks into the square the window makes in front of her, a random selection of the world out there on whose eventfulness she is now depending: a hedge, two palm trees in front of a background that is difficult to disentangle, a sliver of sky in between, above. Her whole attention is focused on this opening, an opening that is not open. She wants to get up, tear open the window, but she cannot even sit up, is separated from the elements out there, separated by the pane. No sound gets through to her, only the noise of the machine in the corner of the room. To hear a bird sing now, a passing car!

Anne closes her eyes; she remembers the story that Emilio once told her, one he began the way he always began his stories:

> ...Once upon a time there was a physicist, who conscientiously sought to explore the world in a physical manner. Until one beautiful summer's day, this intelligent and serious man stood in his garden, just stood there for a while and breathed and looked. The balmy wind stroked his skin softly, the flowers gave off their scent lavishly, reveled in their colorfulness, the birds caroled, the insects whizzed, buzzed around him, and the whole thing seemed like the universe was dancing.
>
> The scientists closed his eyes. Time seemed

to stand still, the line between him and everything around him blurred, he had the feeling he was entering into a relationship that was taking place everywhere at once, the feeling of being one with the cosmos.

The intelligent man had heard about such things from the mystics.

-"What have I got to do with the mystics?" he thought confoundedly and continued to contemplate everything even more seriously and more conscientiously.

It is night. The hot winds have died away, the nurse comes and opens the window, cool darkness enters.

…And he came to the conclusion that what he had experienced could not have been like this in reality: There was neither light nor color, neither scents nor bird song; the whole sensory world only seemed to exist. Instead, the world was composed of a few elements that moved in black, cold silence and were in a strange state of dependency, sometimes in fleeting relation to one another, sometimes in more steady relation, in some places more or less coherent, yes, he was convinced of it now and wrote a new book…"

Anne breathes in the fresh, aromatic air. She feels better.

8. *The German Doctor*

Anne sits in the shadow of her hotel's front garden patio and stares through the flower hedges at the sea, three days until departure, an eternity. Her body holds no tension, the harbor encloses her like a vacuum in which she no longer knows how to move. Sitting next to the entrance is a guest in a wheelchair, also gazing towards the sea. He's drinking a beer, a movement which he manages fairly well with his left hand, he can turn his head slightly, too, but otherwise he's paralyzed; a waiter checks on him every now and then, stops next to him, takes the white cloth off his arm, shakes it out a bit, puts it back again neatly folded, clears his throat and smiles encouragingly at the invalid, *bueno*.

The paralytic has a casual attractiveness, like a racecar driver after an accident. Two English men come up to him, pat his shoulder, laugh cheerily, move along, he laughs back – a brief, throaty laugh – then he looks over to Anne.

- I could just go and sit with him, Anne thinks, but just then she notices an older gentleman with a straw hat approaching her, wheeling a lady's bicycle. It's her bicycle. Until this moment she hadn't asked for it, hadn't even thought about it. The gentleman stops in front of her.

"So it was you who saved my life? My name is Anne, Anne Berghaus..." she says, gets up and extends her hand.

"Well, I have to say I am a doctor, but it was primarily my air-conditioned car that helped you," the man responds graciously and parks the bicycle. He asks Anne how she's doing, more than politeness resonating in his question.

"Still a bit weak, but please do take a seat!"

The waiter brings another glass of water.

"What on earth were you thinking, riding your bike in this weather?" the stranger continues, his voice stern. Something in the man's face makes her trust him.

"I don't know, I really don't know."

"Is this your first time on the island? " he asks.

"No, no, I've known Majorca for many years," Anne replies quickly.

He looks at her intently.

"Where are you from?"

"Berlin."

He laughs.

"Are you from Berlin, too?" Anne enquires.

"Yes, but I've been living here for a long time now."

The waiter brings the water.

"Excuse me, what was your name again?" Anne asks.

"It was like a calling, you know," he says, without responding to her question. "I once witnessed a tragic misdiagnosis here; the story affected me strongly at the time, and other things too, as time went on, but since then I've wanted to settle here." He takes a sip of water, leans back. "It was early February, during the almond blossom season, my wife and I were sitting in the Bar Español in the afternoon like we normally do, drinking our Cortado, when we heard the wailing of ambulance sirens; there was a big to-do in the bar, somebody came and frantically asked me for help, the people knew that I was a doctor. Shortly afterwards I was standing in front of a young man's bed, he was in his early thirties, he had a bad case of pneumonia and was already in a coma; the old village Medico had been treating him for kidney inflammation all this time, it was too late to help, the young man died on his way to Palma…"

Anne grows pale as he recalls the story, she clasps her hands together.

"I'm sorry if I've upset you with this," the doctor says.

"That was Emilio, my husband..." Anne says softly, her voice is shaky.

"Oh my god...!" The doctor takes her in his arms, Anne closes her eyes. Memories well up inside her: She sees Emilio being carried out of the bedroom, down the narrow stairs, slowly, step by step, the house dark, cold and wet, the new heaters were supposed to be installed soon, the gas heaters were not enough, always the stench of butanol, many people in front of the house, a neighbor puts a shawl around her, takes little Pablo and walks with him over to the other children...

Anne gets up, brushes her hair out of her face.

"I thought I had gotten over this a long time ago."

"That kind of pain fuses with our cell tissue," the doctor says quietly and fills up her water. "Are you alright?"

"Yes, thanks, I'm okay." Anne takes a sip of water.

"You know, all our thoughts and feelings are stored somewhere in our systems. They can have a negative impact on chemical processes, even create toxins, which weaken the body and lead to disease," the doctor explains, his eyes fixed on Anne.

"Is there no end? I mean, will I always be weakened by it?"

"Maybe this accident will help you to finally come to terms with the whole thing…For now you need to rest, I'll let you be."

"Wait, sorry, can I ask you something else? Is your wife actually happy here, I mean, is there anything she misses?"

"My wife? She was really looking forward to Majorca. But she didn't live to experience it." He gets up. "If you don't mind, I'd like to come by again tomorrow. When are you flying back?"

"The day after tomorrow."

"Here's my address. You can call me anytime if you need anything. That's what I'm here for," the doctor says.

Anne thanks him, he says goodbye, turns once again, Anne waves, puts the business card away: Dr. Paul Hagemann. Hagemann? The name seems familiar.

A young man picks the paralytic up for a ride. Anne goes back to her room.

Marie II

And Nothing Happens In Isolation

_______*And Nothing Happens In Isolation*

Ringing. The heart stumbles into a faster pace. A queasy feeling tugs inside the stomach. Lying in bed, incredibly heavy, puffy, putrescent in the mouth. Turn over. Keep sleeping. No, get up, otherwise it's just going to get worse.

The phone is ringing. I cannot speak right now. It's good that I'm alone. A *good morning* from anyone and I would flee into the farthest corner of the apartment, the bathroom! As it is, I shuffle to it at my own pace, my eyes barely open. Looking in the mirror brings no clarity whatsoever. I recognize myself in the reflection with the consciousness of an ape. The shower helps. It might be the cool jet of water or the room temperature that is just below body heat: The body that had come apart at the seams shiveringly contracts and takes on its normal form. Heart and circulation obey, adjust to being vertical. While drying off, the body parts are polished, the skin reacts with more color, and the second glance in the mirror is less disconcerting. Putting on some lotion, using the comb, and putting on the dressing gown allow some sense of familiarity to resurface. I move into the kitchen and continue to stabilize while making coffee: rinsing the glass carafe, pouring in the water, wrinkling up the filter paper, dipping the measuring spoon into the blackish-brown mass, closing the lid, switching it *on*, then the prompt seething of water dripping and the aromatic fumes, finally the cup of coffee, clouded golden with cream, a glance at the clock and my consciousness confirms:

-I am drinking coffee in my kitchen at ten o'clock.

And just imagine what would happen if I were to suddenly observe: The dark-haired woman of indefinable age is drinking coffee in her apartment at ten o'clock in the morning. Then this self would be utterly lost. Luckily, there is no doubt now: I can feel my lips touching the china; my mucous membranes experience the hot liquid, and these are my gastric juices that rejoice in meeting my beloved poison; my gullet channeling the brownish trickle down, leaving behind a warm trail in my stomach.

I light a cigarette, suck on the filter of the lit stick, and breathe in the slowly searing herb. The fumes blend with the flowing parts of my body, then, in a transformed state, penetrate my brain, and effect sensual tension, a readiness for concentration and activity.

The phone is ringing again. The answering machine has been turned down. It is probably my mother. Or Christian. I don't feel like speaking.

> The day was very long; the mother left the house early in the morning and didn't return until evening. When the girl finally heard the key in the lock, she was happy and would have loved to have flung her arms around her mother's neck. But she knew that the mother disliked this. She was exhausted after the strenuous day and had little time. The child understood this and was careful to formulate her questions and answers quickly and precisely.
>
> Things must not go wrong, otherwise the mother would get angry and that was unthinkable. The girl talked about her day quickly, that she had read, slept, and done her school work, that the thermometer still read 100.4°, and at the same time assured her mother that she was feeling much better already.
>
> In the meantime, the mother was running

back and forth, had taken off, put down, unpacked, and put things away, peeled the potatoes, turned on the oven, put the potatoes on, and put oil in the pan for the meat. The salad still had to be washed. The girl's narrative stabbed her stomach; she did not dare look into the pale little face. The child had been home alone for two weeks already. Pain and bitterness tormented the mother equally. Most of the time, the bitterness prevailed. After all, it was not her fault that she had to work all day. They gave her a run for her money there. She briefly went to the girl's bed.

"Can you eat in the kitchen? That would be easier."

"Oh yes," the child said.

- This god-awful sadness even when she's happy, the mother thought of her little girl. What the doctor had told her recently. "Your daughter is unusually sensitive. Her body, spirit, and soul are very closely entwined; you have to take extra care of her!"

"What does that mean?" she asked him.

"Well, how should I explain this..." And he ended up giving no explanation at all, at least she didn't understand what he was saying, only felt a silent assignment of guilt.

- So what, other children have to cope with things too, the mother thought. Sometimes there just wasn't any feeling left. After all she was no cow that could be milked for love. She felt dried out inside, she was only functioning, had to function.

"Mrs. Hamacher asked about you again. She wanted to know what you've been up to all day, and whether you were terribly bored all on your own," the mother said when they were both sitting at the table.

"I told her that you never get bored," she continued, not without pride in the little girl who showed aptitude in all subjects at school and was extraordinarily studious and eager to learn; pride also in herself because she was impressive as a single mother with an illegitimate child.

My eye disengages from the kitchen, becomes available to look outside. I open the door to the kitchen balcony. Blue sky, swallows gliding, the thousand-fold green of the maple and chestnut trees hiding the windows of the houses across the way, framing the visible red of their rooftops. In the flower boxes marguerite daisies, rosemary, and moss rose grow rampant. Bumblebees have bombarded the lavender pot. They sniff and taste the fragrant blossoms tirelessly. I sit down at the kitchen table and enjoy my successful presence within myself on this summer day, in the city of Berlin, in the heart of Europe, on the brink of the third millennium. I have found myself and at the same time a world around me with which I had been involved before I even became aware it.

The child was often sick; then she would receive a special kind of attention from her working mother and was excused from her chores for a while. This was not a calculated move on the child's part. She was indeed seriously ill every time and would lie home alone for weeks, next to her a little table with gruel, medicine, tissues, a clinical thermometer, and a clock by which she promptly took her drops and pills; books and dolls all around her. She especially liked to read from the big old book of Grimms' Fairy Tales, which was over a thousand pages long. There were many fairy tales in it that nobody knew. The girl must have read them all well over a hundred times, but to her they seemed to be more wonderful every time. When she was exhausted from reading, she took a doll into her arms and fell asleep with a vague sense of longing.

Midmorning once again demonstrates the validity of a lot of physical, chemical, and biological insights. The earth is turning properly, gravitation is steadily effective, the sun is warming the earth and gives its light from its place, the plants assimilate carbon dioxide and release oxygen, the static of the house has proven itself - it is still standing; the electricity cools, warms, and moves as planned; no doubt, the world is in working order, the whole universe is in solidarity this morning, just like any other, and I am right in the middle of it.

I go to sit outside on the small kitchen balcony. Elements of light, warmth, and sounds take me in to their loose, elastic nexus. My perception is very close to these things. I feel the world's physical operations.

An old neighbor went to look after her from time to time; she liked the child but the mother was not fond of her. She hated the poor woman. It was probably only the smell of garlic that constantly enveloped the old woman because the mother hated garlic, too.

Occasionally however, the girl was allowed to visit the woman, and they would play rummy. At the old woman's place it always smelled of urine and Eau de Cologne, and the little one didn't think there was any other way it could be. The child was touched by the woman's clown-like ugliness; her beady, lashless eyes were always swimming tears. Sometimes her granddaughter would come to visit from East Berlin, and the three of them would play cards on the round table with the colorful waxen table cloth and there would be crumble cake; it felt cozy.

One Christmas Eve, the old woman's daughter-in-law and granddaughter stood under the window in front of the house in the middle of the night screaming loudly: the youngest son had just been killed in an accident. One could hear the women's desperate wails next door until the morning. From that point on, the old woman was confused. One day they came to take her away. The child never saw her again.

Doors are banging shut. The garbage collectors are

on their way. They cart the trash bins into the yard, the full ones back to the street. The little wheels of the garbage truck rattle loudly over the bumpy, cobbled street. The final bin exchanged, the doors fall shut.

It's Monday. The bins are also emptied on Wednesdays and Fridays, but today it is Monday; the special sobriety of a Monday morning inside the walls of the house.

> Sometimes the mother was sick, that was bad because the mother only stayed home when she couldn't go on, and the child was terribly afraid that her mother might die. On the other hand, it was nice to have her mother to herself for once and to see her lying there so relaxed and peaceful, yes, she felt that despite the fever, stomach cramps, and biliary colics, the mother was actually grateful to be able to lie in bed; her voice was very soft then, a gentle glint in her eyes.

Everything had been different the day before: All morning long, the block of houses sank under the constant waves of the Sunday chimes' vibrations, which came from all four directions; bold reminders of transcendence from the nearby churches.

In the afternoon there had been a party in the house next door, the sounds of dishes, glasses, voices, and pop music spilled over; the young woman downstairs was constantly listening to Brian Adams's *Please Forgive Me.* Last week she had had a fight with her girlfriend, the door had been kicked in. The custodian said that women were worse than men in that way, while leaving open what he meant with "in that way." At lunchtime there had been the delicious smell of roast lamb, garlic, and rosemary, later on of freshly baked cake. The custodian's children played in the sandbox and rode their tricycles around the trees, making engine noises. Somewhere a man and a woman were fighting. The man was yelling. When he paused, the woman would counter calmly, like the forte and piano in a concerto grosso, permeated by a girl's thin, sobbing voice. I do not know these people. In the freshly renovated apartment above me, the newlywed couple was audibly making love with the window wide open, on the roof terrace Frank, the hairdresser, revels in a tango. Mrs. Beyer's apartment, diagonally below, is still empty.

The girl was about five years old when she went to visit her relatives in the Uckermark. The cousin had just had a baby; the child was allowed to sit with the baby on an armchair in the living room, and then she felt very happy.

Once, on a very warm summer's day when the girl was sitting alone like this again, cuddling the newborn, the gold of the corn fields was shining through the wide-open window into the living room and the heat stifled everything. Then a strange weakness befell the girl. The pounding of her heart resonated through her whole body, she felt faint, she felt numb, baring her little chest, she pressed the baby's little face to her and with her free hand felt for the spot where the blood was pulsating most strongly. She rubbed and kneaded until she was exhausted and her limbs had become so heavy she had trouble holding the sleeping bundle. When the girl returned home, she tried to repeat the experience with her doll. Shaking, she lay down next to it, and more and more rapidly she managed to bring her body to exhaustion. Every time the lust overwhelmed the girl, she would feel an aimless desire and sadness afterwards, the pain of which would make her cry.

I go into my room, get dressed, stand in front of the mirror. The tight jeans fit closely over my stomach and rear, the deeply plunging black top accentuates my breasts.

"Your body is like milk and honey," Rudolf had raved.

The phone is ringing again. Probably my mother. Sometimes she can't come up with a word in her crossword puzzle: "Marie, you with your education must know this!" Then always the same disappointment:

"That you don't know something like this! I only have my O-levels, but back then we got a general education..."

She ended up cancelling the bus tour to Switzerland because she received a letter from her brother-in-law Karl from Vienna, her secret infatuation, a dapper man in his late seventies whose wife is in a wheelchair. Since Fritz, Mother's last husband, had died last year, a correspondence started up between Berlin and Vienna, which offensively exceeded any permissible affinity by marriage. There were a few things to resolve about the inheritance. She had already received a golden signet ring in the mail, and Karl, for his part, did not seem disinclined to get to know his brother's vibrant wife a little better.

"What do you think, should I just write that I'll come or wait until they invite me? You could put me on a train at Zoo Station; I won't need much luggage. Just for a few days. Vienna is a wonderful city!" Mother exclaimed and decided to buy a new blouse for her ladies' suit; one always looks dressed up in a suit. But a few days later she sounded despondent, she didn't have the courage to go after all. Of course she wanted to stay in the brother-in-law's house; but if the sister-in-law wouldn't let her then she would have to find a hotel. But she wanted to see Karl. After all, the woman is still alive, she owns the house, too, and she wasn't stupid. So the mother wrote another letter to the in-laws.

One night the girl woke up with a fright. Noise. Robbers, she thought as she silently climbed out of bed and tiptoed to the door. She reached the hallway without a sound, saw the mother's shape at the open apartment door. When the mother noticed the child, she closed the door, angrily came up to the little one, and slapped her in the face: What was she thinking, secretly spying on her mother in the middle of the night? For a long time the girl lay awake crying and thinking about what she had done wrong. The mother didn't mention the incident in the morning, nor in

> the days to follow, and in the end the little girl believed it had all been a dream.

I walk back into the kitchen, pour myself the rest of the coffee, go to sit outside again. A new day lies ahead of me, the possibility of creating a new reality. To fill every moment with awareness: That would be it. Searching for meaning: Nothing essential anywhere. Searching for a reason that carries and enables unity, unity between things, the cosmos and myself: anything else, Madame...

My consciousness is awake now, insists on continuity. It is summer, Johannes has gone on vacation with Christian, and Anne has flown to Mallorca on the spur of the moment. My legs have healed well, last night I even went dancing in Far-Out; rock, pop, hip-hop, in between the Sanyassin-trance-techno-house droning, whatever, good atmosphere, excitement, sensual enjoyment galore, a dark-skinned man got a round of applause in the middle of the dance floor and a drink on the house; he stood next to me with a cocktail, he liked my way of dancing, yes, I just loved to dance, and what about him? He was a dancer, currently involved with the Theatre of the West, didn't I want to drink with him, and the glass was already in my hand; the stuff tasted good but I just cannot stomach alcohol; we stayed until the end, then the usual. No. Ciao, Bello. The birds were chirping, the morning chastely edged up over the sleeping city, and I fell heavily into bed.

At the age of nine, the girl wrote her first book. The protagonist was Unti, a popular boy from the day care who overpowered screaming girls during games of robbers and princesses, tying them to trees, touching them up, and kissing them. Taboo words were strung together, the meaning of which the girl did not understand, the ring of them aroused her, the whole thing illustrated with stereotypical half-naked female bodies with big breasts. It must have been some kind of scandal when the teacher caught the girl covertly showing her scribblings to a friend; the girl was taken to task by the adults for weeks. Since she was considered to be a good girl, they believed her innocence and tried to sound her out for the true creator of the dirty pictures. They couldn't find anyone to blame, and eventually they dropped the whole thing.

The telephone again. Now I answer.

“Hello!”

“Marie, finally! I’ve been trying to reach you for the umpteenth time, why weren’t you answering the phone?”

My mother, she sounds tense.

“I’m sorry, I wasn’t ready.”

“All you have to do is pick up the receiver and talk to your mother, how ready do you have to be?”

The conversation wasn’t off to a good start.

“So what are you up to?” she asks slyly.

“I’m drinking coffee...”

“It’s almost 11 a.m.!”

“I slept in today...”

“Have you heard anything from Johannes yet? Did you have to send the poor child on vacation with Christian and this weird Uschi person?” she interrupts me while I am trying to gain a foothold in the undergrowth of her petulance:

“What’s wrong, Mamá?” even though she finds Mamá with a stress on the last syllable silly; I just cannot bring myself to say mommy.

“Ah, well, you could call me from time to time, too; I’m always bothering you. I’m not well. Have no appetite. My stomach...” All at once her voice is soft, and a confiding report about her physical state pours out. “Can’t you cook something nice for me today at my place, carrot stew?"

My mother, who does not like to ask for anything, is strangely urgent, different than usual. I haven't seen her for a long time and feel happy at the thought of taking this stubborn little person into my arms, even though it's never been easy; she could never accept tenderness at all.

"Alright, I'll be there around one."

"Drive carefully!" she says and hangs up.

Downstairs in the hall I meet the custodian's young wife. She looks haggard. Her white complexion, which usually lends her an almost consumptive beauty, today only makes her appear ill.

"My lower back, I can hardly move," she groans, one hand on her back, while her gaze wanders over my body and stops at my cleavage.

"I'm sorry to hear that, it's such a beautiful day today, the sun..." My sentences subside of their own accord.

"Sun? It's only you up there who gets it. We sit with the lights on all summer. The trees block out everything. It's lighter in the winter, well, but then it's also cold. And four people in the small apartment, with the little one running around already." Her eyes are stuck at my naked feet in the sandals.

Could I bring her anything?

"No, no, my husband's taking care of me."

I wish her a speedy recovery, turn to go.

"Oh, by the way, the rats in the cellar are getting more and more feisty, the little critters. The house management has to do something, will you sign the petition, too?"

"Yes, of course."

"Well, then..." The young woman disappears into her apartment. I take my bike, ride to the supermarket.

Once, when the child went shopping with the mother and was waiting for her in front of the store, she saw another girl about the same age. They looked at each other, and the child felt that this was a special moment: both waiting outside for their mothers.

-This has to mean something, she thought excitedly and smiled at the strange girl, yes, she liked her already. All the things they could do together: play with dolls, play hide and seek, play ball, share all their secrets!

"Should we be friends?" the words toppled out of the girl's mouth and her eyes were shining, her heart felt very warm. But the strange child just looked away, turned around.

> The girl suddenly felt as if there were a hole in her chest, and was ashamed.

I buy spare ribs, carrots, parsley, and a plump, wonderfully shiny aubergine for myself for tomorrow. In front of me at the checkout is a woman with a little boy; he is holding a bar of chocolate in his hand, peeks up at me.

"You have to put this on the belt first," says the woman.

"I know, Grandma."

The little one lifts the bar up, a new brand of chocolate that's supposed to give you wings when you eat it. The boy snuggles up to the woman's body.

"Grandma, can you really fly if you eat this chocolate?"

"Nah." The grandmother looks irritably at the cashier who is threatening to fall asleep with each item she drags across the belt. The little one presses the chocolate with the flying person on the wrapper to his body.

"Yes, Grandma, when you eat this chocolate then you get a tingling feeling in your stomach and it goes whee just like you're flying!"

"Yes, yes, of course." The woman strokes his head. The little one looks at me triumphantly.

My turn. The young cashier is new here, visible thought processes accompany her movements. Behind me, the line is growing. The aubergine has to be keyed in separately, the young woman searches in vain for the article on the price list.

"What are these things called?"

"Aubergines: 5.99 DM per kilo…" I utter.

"No, I need a number," she says and engrosses herself in the list again. "Well, they're definitely not under O." Red spots appear on her neck.

"With A-u," I add quietly.

"Oh, I see."

"Where in the world is she from?" somebody shouts from the back.

When the girl was thirteen, Rudi moved in. Rudi had spent mornings sitting in the same commuter train compartment as the mother for quite a while now; but Rudi was as good-looking as he was shy, and the mother did not dare speak to him, either; thus the rapprochement dragged on until late summer. During that time, the mother got a new dress made from fine, lilac tafetta, interwoven with blossoms, with a tight waist and a wide, pleated skirt. She bought white, elegant suede ballet pumps to go with it, swooshing through the apartment with it from mirror to mirror:

"Well, how do I look?" she asks, enjoying the admiration in the daughter's eyes; her dark brown eyes shone, the full, black hair lying in soft waves around her small face.

Finally, one morning, when the train was especially shaky and creaky, Rudi said loudly:

"What is this, a train or a swing set?" and they smiled at each other. The mother took care of the rest. Rudi moved in, bought a new vacuum, and vacuumed the whole apartment on a regular basis; it was a man's job, he said; he also brought in the heavy stuff, potatoes, beer, flavored sparkling water; he read his paper in silence and otherwise did not interfere with things.

"We live together," the mother explained to the daughter. "And if somebody asks you who Rudi is, then you'll say he's Daddy."

Daddy of course had a real wife, she lived behind the station and exerted various pressures on the self-proclaimed couple, thereby invoking her rights after twenty-five dutiful years of marriage. Meanwhile, the mother jealously guarded her new love's bliss, in equal measures feared and hated the wife in the far-away part of Zehlendorf. Rudi had to swear to never return to her again. That went well for a while. But the mother's periodic outbursts of rage came from out of the blue, and her intellectual superiority and unsurpassable eloquence proved to be too much for the poor man, who actually only longed for peace and quiet. He tried to escape several times, but in these crises, mostly on weekends, the mother would lock herself into the bathroom or the kitchen, threaten to jump out of the window or turn on the gas tap and blow everything up. Every time this happened, the girl was terribly afraid, stood in front of the door crying and begging her mother not to do anything bad, while Daddy retreated into the living room. Fortunately, most of these dramas ended quite quickly, and afterwards they would eat dinner peacefully, the three of them together.

One beautiful warm Friday in July when he had taken a day off work, Rudi managed to escape after all. When the mother came home, his things were gone, the apartment strangely empty. The mother remained composed and went with her now sixteen year-old daughter to get some ice cream. Over a delicious fruit sundae they agreed that it was much better to live without a man anyway. Later on, the mother married Hermann, but the girl had already moved out.

My mother lives in Britz, in a bright, newly built apartment on the fourth floor, with a view over fields and gardens. In the summer she spends the whole day on the balcony, surrounded by bright red geraniums. She works on crossword puzzles there, cleans vegetables, sews, and does her nails; the TV guide always within reach, on the windowsill the coffeepot with the big felt poodle cozy. My mother's complexion is always beautiful; a few sunrays and she looks like she just had three weeks' vacation in the South. The last time her skin had seemed rather white, well, it had been cold and rainy. I drive across the expressway, get off at Geradestraße, through lush avenues, past the Neukölln Hospital, park in the tenants' parking lot, ring the doorbell three times, no answer, again, finally the door opener buzzes. I take the elevator up, look forward to the pointy, curious face in the open doorway and the usual welcome ceremony:

"Come on in then, alright, alright, close the door, not everybody has to hear everything..." Her excited pacing back and forth and her questions, what would I like to eat, she had made a leavened cake especially for me, a big piece of cheesecake was still in the freezer, should she go ahead and defrost it or give it to me later to take home. Then we would sit down on the balcony and she would say: "Tell!"

I would talk about the logic-lecturer from the university, who's divorced – wouldn't that be the kind of man for you? – and about the seminar on the philosophy of the Romantic period; ah, the Romantic! She loves Klopstock and Kleist, and what was the name of this very young female poet, yes, the Günderode, who always carried a knife with her and dreamed of one day thrusting it into her heart, and then she actually went and did it! Goethe, with all due respect, was not her thing, he had just had too good a life, but she admired Schiller all the more, he had had to fight hard for everything...

I step out of the elevator, no head in the doorframe, the door closed. I ring the bell, Mrs. Weber, the neighbor, opens the door.

"Where's my mother?"

"Your mother called me earlier. She just couldn't manage on her own anymore. It's no wonder, she hasn't been eating for weeks, she hasn't had an appetite, she says. She told me you were about to come over, she didn't say anything to you? You really have to go to a doctor with her! It's urgent! She keeps spitting everything up!"

I rush to my mother's bed, stop aghast; her face has become smaller and very pale.

"I brought carrots and spare ribs..." I fight back tears.

"Everything keeps coming back up," she says in a weak voice and swallows hard.

"Then I'll first make our gruel soup, it's always helped, remember?" I try to sound cheery.

"Yes, with nothing in it."

Mrs. Weber leaves. I cook the oatmeal without milk or sugar, just with water and a pinch of salt, pour it into a colorful little bowl, lay out spoon and napkin, bring the tray to my mother's bed, sit down next to her. She takes a small spoonful of the stuff, swallows laboriously.

"Don't worry, mommy, I'll feed you, we've got time."

"No, no, no chance..." She feebly sinks back into the pillows, closes her eyes...

> … "It's a girl, a beautiful, healthy girl!" she hears the night nurse say.

She was miserably exhausted by the birth, the hardships, lonely, left alone in the bitter winter, without hope, without future.

"So what do you want to name her?" the nurse asks again and again.

Of course, the child was supposed to be named Wolfgang. After all, she wanted a son, a boy that looked like Paul...She had no name for this being here...Paul, where are you – I'm waiting for you – Paul, my Paul – your sunny laugh, your dark locks – our son has to look like you, Paul, he has to have your laugh – oh Lord, life could be good again – with you, Paul – when will you come – I can't wait anymore – I'm so afraid – don't be too late, Paul...

"Why don't you call her Maria?" the nurse says and puts the baby into her arms.

"Then rather Marie..." the mother whispers and faints.

Marie calls the ambulance and remains at her mother's bedside.

Dear Anne,

Yes, I've buried my mother. The cancer from her stomach had spread to her esophagus. Pumped full of morphine, in the end she lay there, breathing heavily, her pulse very quick, very small and thin, shrunken in from all sides. I was with her as much as I could be, but I think it was more my need than hers. It's like this: my whole life I loved past this woman somehow, have always missed her. In her estate she left a thin, black notebook with irregular entries from when she was pregnant with me. I'm grappling with the fact that I've lost a huge part of my livelihood. I'll be back in touch as soon as I can.

Yours,
Marie

Once upon a time there was a woman
who had a child,
and the child said: Mother, tell me a story.
And so the mother began:
once upon a time there was a woman, a child,
and no man...

PalmArtPress Program

Maria Reinecke
La Rambla -*Barcelona Story*
ISBN: 978-3-941524-02-6 German, 76 Pages
ISBN: 978-3-941524-26-2 D (eBook)
ISBN: 978-3-941524-20-0 English, 96 Pages
ISBN: 978-3-941524-25-5 E (eBook)
Softcover, 12 x 18 cm

Michael Lederer
The Great Game, Das große Spiel
Berlin-Warschau Express und andere Geschichten
ISBN: 978-3-941524-12-5 English, 242 Pages
ISBN: 978-3-941524-13-2 German, 280 Pages
ISBN: 978-3-941524-27-9 G (eBook)
Softcover, 14,8 x 21 cm

Anne Lorquet-Leithäuser
Kirschenzeiten
ISBN: 978-3-941524-17-0
ISBN: 978-3-941524-35-4 (eBook)
288 Pages, Softcover 14,8 x 21 cm

Michael Lederer
Nothing Lasts Forever/ Nichts ist mehr für die Ewigkeit
ISBN: 978-3-941524-33-0 English
ISBN: 978-3-941524-32-3 German
ISBN: 978-3-941524-31-6 G (eBook)
Softcover, 14,8 x 21 cm

Wolfgang Nieblich
Wahr oder Nicht wahr
ISBN: 978-3-941524-14-9
ISBN: 978-3-941524-28-6 (eBook)
266 Pages, Softcover, 12 x 18 cm

Wolfgang Nieblich
Der Hecht im Schulranzen
ISBN: 978-3-941524-08-8
ISBN: 978-3-941524-18-7 (eBook)
192 Pages, 168 Color Illustr.,
Hardcover, 14,8 x 21 cm

Michael Kromarek
KunstGeschichten ***-ernst und heiter***
ISBN: 978-3-941524-11-8
ISBN: 978-3-941524-19-4 (eBook)
150 Pages, Softcover, 12 x 18 cm

Wolfgang Nieblich
Das Ferne so nah oder **Die Currywurst**
ISBN: 978-3-941524-09-5
ISBN: 978-3-941524-29-3 (eBook)
64 Pages, 18 Color Illustr.,
Hardcover, 8 x 10 cm

Sladjana Lukic
Deutsche Grammatik- ***leicht gemacht***
ISBN: 978-3-941524-04-0
216 Pages, Softcover, 16,5 x 23,5 cm